PUNCHLINES

Brent Taylor

-Contents-

PUNCHLINE

A lot of people say to me: Why did you kill Christ? I dunno... It was one of those parties, got out of hand...
   -Lenny Bruce

  1.

A blonde, a brunette, and a redhead walk into a bar looking to buy cocaine... It's the business end of a Saturday night (Sunday morning in the mind of any responsible citizen). We were at the club – at The Rim Shot (or Rim Job, affectionately, because, among more apropos reasons, really how many comedy clubs called The Rim Shot should there be allowed in America). My friend and I had performed earlier at the open mic night, which is always the last Saturday of the month. I think my bit worked. On the other hand, my buddy, my best friend since high school, my junko partna, my co-conspirator, my roommate – he bombed. Once one of the funniest guys I knew, his routine is too philosophical now, too intellectual. Half the audience doesn't understand the words he uses in his latest routine. It's gotten to where he makes these stream-of-consciousness transitions, and he'll do it so smoothly from one point to the other the audience won't notice until later that he's forgotten to tie up an idea he began with.

Tonight, it was a Burma Shave.

What's a Burma Shave anyway? asks this punk rocker in a motorcycle jacket and spiked bi-hawk. This is at the bar, after the show.

A what? my buddy asks, clasping the punk rocker's hand with a dub bag, trading it for a 20 dollar bill.

In your set, you said something about Burma-Shave.

Oh, that.

What the fuck is it?

I could tell you, says my buddy. But then I'd have to kill you.

You? says the punk rocker. Kill *me*?

He had to be 6'4, 250. Why not? my friend says. I'll polish the floor with the brushes on your your head.

Dude, c'mon, I say.

What's a Burma Shave? The punk rocker is angry now.

His buddy, shorter, but very solid, steps up behind him.

And what the fuck is *telemetry*? And *transmigration of souls*?

That's not a joke, the little guy says. This guy's the fucking joke.

Hey, it's cool guys, I say, raise a finger to the bartender to bring the guys a beer. It's nothing.

What is it, then? the big guy says.

It's shaving cream, I tell him. But it's from Lenny Bruce's book. Actually, it's something we misread once from Lenny Bruce. We thought it was a cocktail from a benzadrine inhaler and cocaine, but it was benzadrine and Coca-Cola. And it wasn't even called a Burma Shave, that was just a sign he saw earlier in the paragraph or something. We misread it, and it's become an inside joke.

I knew it, the big guy said. Lenny Bruce. I knew I'd read that shit somewhere.

He looks at his friend, back at me.

It's not funny, though, he says.

I shrug, and they take their beers.

That's when these three women walk in, probably in their middle or late thirties, almost certainly divorcees given the absence of a ring on all but one of their left ring fingers. *A blonde, a brunette, and a redhead walk into a bar looking to buy cocaine...* The redhead was separated I supposed, or at least not worried about the sizable diamond on her finger in relation to how she associated with strange men. Maybe it was a bachelorette party, maybe something else – who am I to ask questions? Some nights just have a way of getting ahead of themselves.

2.

I slam on the brakes, but it's too late – there's a thud punctuated by the sound of screeching tires. It's after 3 am, so we can sit there in the middle of the road catching our breath. I had knocked my head on something hard where my hand on the steering wheel should have been.

I saw the handcuffs still locked on my wrist.

What the fuck was that? I shout.

It was a dog, man! A fucking dog!

I didn't even see it! What the hell!

It just ran out into the middle of the street! It was wandering on the side, he says. I almost said something.

Why the fuck didn't you?

I didn't know it would dart out! We have to check on it.

Check on it? It's dead! We hit it straight on!

Maybe not... we have to make sure.

I'm sure!

Look, what if it's in pain, he says. Just lying there, waiting for another car to come along and wipe it out?

What are we going to do with it if it's alive? What if a cop comes along?

We tell him what happened.

Tell him, what? We were going up to the store to get more beer at 2 o'clock in the morning? That we ran over a stupid dog, but because it was stupid, not because we were drunk?

He doesn't answer.

I'll let you handle that one, I say.

3.

Stop me if you've heard this one. No, really, hold me down. Save me some trouble, some embarrassment. Handcuffs, maybe? I promise I'm not really into kinky shit – not unless you want me to be. The thing is – and maybe this is just me trying to make sense of random events, trying to make it into something other than that dreaded rim shot after a bad joke before the not-laughter – the thing is: maybe you never actually wake up as who you want to be in the morning. And maybe, just maybe, at some point, you learn the hard way that you have to be okay with that, or else you're always going to take it out on yourself and those around you in one way or another.

That particular night, I was taking it out on myself and those around me. We were getting drunk at the bar at the club after open mic night, when *a blonde, a brunette, and a redhead walk into a bar looking to buy cocaine...* No joke. You can't make this shit up if you tried. On the night in question – at the time in question – it so happens my roommate and I were gainfully employed in a small business in which we sold cocaine for personal consumption at the bar of said club. The Rim Job, we'll call it. We had just re-upped earlier in the day for the coming week. The only problem: it's not broken up because it's Saturday, the night before Easter Sunday, and even though it's open mic night and usually a pretty good turnout, we didn't quite expect such a demand. Nonetheless, at that point, it was looking like even Jesus would be wishing he was stoned this Sunday morning coming down...

So when the brunette approaches me at the bar to see what I've got, I've just sold my last dub bag, and the main stash is back at the house for safe-keeping.

I shrug. Did you catch my set? I ask her, changing the subject.

Would you know anyone else here that might be able to do us a favor? she says, and I look over at my partner. He downs a shot of Jameson's. After briefly debating with our eyes whether or not I can get away with asking the last customer for the dub back, we have the brilliant idea to invite the girls back to our place for a beer. Granted, it violates nearly every rule we set for ourselves when we started our aforementioned business, seeing as one has to be careful in one's dealings when exchanging goods and services traditionally reserved for men's rooms and back alleys. But still, any good business plan has to adapt to changing markets.

Or as my partner put it, leaning over to talk directly into my ear: These girls are fine, man.

Having always had a thing for women a decade or so older than me, in spite having a perfectly loving mother (albeit slightly white wine and Xanax dependent), I shrugged. Let it be known, ladies and gentlemen, I have never once discriminated based on age or race.

We can definitely help you out, I say.

4.

Oh shit, it's alive...

The dog is lying there, curled, looking back like we've come to finish it off. It's brown or gray, difficult to tell in the amber light of the streetlamps, but it's long-haired, with pointy ears, very shaggy.

Why is it shaking like that?

I don't know... maybe because it got hit by a fucking car?

We have to do something.

Like what? Take it to a hospital? It's a dog!

Surely there's an all-night vet somewhere.

I don't even know where a daytime vet is.

This was in the days before smart phones, at least prior to their ubiquity. We didn't even carry cell phones because we were afraid someone would think we were significant enough to tap them.

There's a place over on Highland, he says. My sister takes her dog there.

How do we know it's even open? Hell, how do we get it there?

We put it in the car and take it there.

It'll bleed all over the car.

Man, it's just a fucking car!

Some would argue it's just a fucking dog

5.

Next thing I know, I'm driving my roommate's Sebring convertible because he's too drunk to drive. It's March and still cold out at night, but we put the top down on it out of some unacknowledged and ridiculous attempt to impress the women following us in their car. We're blasting The Replacements at top volume as we blur by all the quiet, safe little houses, and once again, I feel the night getting ahead of itself – like it just ran the yellow light we should have stopped at.

That's when he reaches over and turns down the music.

You want to know the worst thing I've ever done? he says.

Not really, I tell him, already knowing where it's going. I realize then that he's more wasted than I thought. I reach to turn the volume back up, but he grabs my hand.

When I was 20, I took 200 hundred dollars out of my mom's purse.

C'mon, let's just have fun tonight, I tell him. Worry about it tomorrow.

I check in the rearview to make sure the girls are still behind us. They were in a white SUV.

I never told anyone this, he says, not even you.

You told me this two weeks ago when you were wasted, remember?

She was with that rich guy, Bill, at the time, he says.

Come on, man...

It's not like she needed it. I mean, my mom's never carried around that much cash, before or since.

Lately, our other job, the one that's profitable, is starting to get to him. He started selling blow a year and a half ago when his car broke down, and he didn't have the money to fix it. He had been performing at The Rim Job for a little while, was starting to book some off-nights beyond the open mic. Of the two of us, he was the one starting to gain a small audience, in spite of his near-debilitating stage fright. Thus, the cocaine and the booze. Then, he'd met a guy who had a good price on weight, his car was still broken down, and he figured he'd just do it for a few months just to get his car fixed. But a few months and car repairs turned into six months and a new car. Now it's been a year and a half of making the kind of money that can buy you a new car in six months by just going to bars, and he's starting to wonder what it's going to take to get him to quit.

I warned him.

The only thing more addictive than doing cocaine is selling it, I told him, shortly after he started.

I had made this mistake once before, in my early 20's. Not only do you have an ever increasingly expensive cocaine habit, but you get used to throwing money around. Of late, our bank had been dwindling and we were living re-up to re-up, gone from getting ahead to barely keeping up. It's exhausting to live this way, but that's where the blow comes back into it, and before you know it, it's always there.

He doesn't say any of this, but he thinks it. And it's made him quieter. More cerebral. Not a great thing for a comedian or a cocaine dealer. Seriously, I was afraid for a minute he was on smack until I remembered how sick it made him the time we snorted it. Not to mention how his brother had died of an OD when my buddy was still at home – it wrecked his parents' marriage and lives in front of his face.

Always a healthy dose of hapless (as any funny man should be) – I think the seriousness of it is weighing on him. It's hard to spin through life out of control. We all need our white lies to not have to face the truth about ourselves. I mean, no shit, he tried to call his mom to borrow some money for rent about six months ago after he'd blown his bank on this girl he dated for six weeks, buying her a necklace and earrings, and throwing a three day party for his birthday. He couldn't get his mom to call him back. He had to message her on Myspace. No shit. She said she didn't check voicemails anymore. This woman, whose hair he held back from the toilet countless times when she was drunk. He had to take work-study to graduate high school his last year.

She never got him the money, his mom, her latest boyfriend was a cop, and she didn't have it. Instead, I loaned him the money for a re-up, and we turned it into rent.

What's worse, now he's getting paranoid.

The cocaine, no doubt.

But he even tried to start carrying a gun. It was a revolver of some kind, he couldn't even tell me the caliber.

What the fuck is this? I said.

He'd bent over to pick something up, and I saw it in his waistband.

Protection, he told me.

Protection, from what? ...*We're white people in America*

Dude, that's not funny.

I looked at him. If I'd known shit about guns, I would have pistol-whipped him.

What? he'd said.

What?? What, me? What you, mother-fucker! You're the one knocking over liquor stores.

A few months prior, he'd gotten in trouble for fishing the receipt for a stereo out of a trash can at Walmart and then trying to go return the merchandise. A real crackhead scheme, one I know he learned from my ex-girlfriend before she finally went to jail for good.

Aw, come on, he said. You know I couldn't pull a gun on someone.

You just pulled one on me!

Oh fuck you, you know what I mean. I couldn't unless it was self-defense.

Dude, haven't you ever heard of Chekhov's gun? ... I might have meant Murphy's Law, but it was close enough.

I could see him thinking, trying to remember the creative writing class we signed up for at the community college a couple of years back.

Like self-fulfilling prophesy, right? he said.

No, I told him. Forget it. Just fucking google some shit next time before you do something dumb like buying a gun!

I made him give it to me, the gun, said I'd get rid of it. Fortunately, that was the end of it, at least I hoped.

It's worse when he's drunk though, his melancholia. He gets all sentimental about the friends who don't answer his calls anymore, the other friends who only call him for blow. Eventually, he goes off the rails and starts in on this masochistic self-persecution trip where he makes like he's the worst person in the world, not just another guy getting by.

I'd never even done drugs at the time, he says, still going on about his mom. It wasn't for drugs. You'd have to be a real lowlife to steal from your mom over drugs. No, I lost my job delivering pizzas, and I needed to pay rent.

I don't answer him, hoping he'll leave it alone.

It's this next turn up here, he says, pointing out our neighborhood to me.

I start to say something, then decide to ignore it, check my rearview to see the blonde, the brunette, and the redhead are behind us. Again, some sort of white SUV, not brand new, but within the last few years. The brunette is driving. They follow me into the neighborhood.

He's just not cut out for selling cocaine, that's the thing. Not only is he doing too much of his own shit, he spends cash like he's in a strip club. More fundamental than that, it's just not in his philosophical wiring that a guy can make the kind of money he's making for doing essentially nothing. His brain, like every other middle class deadbeat whose parents insisted a liberal arts education would be worth a damn (*Just get the degree, kids! It'll open doors!*), has been infected by the myth of hard work. Easy money just keeps him asking himself if it's finally the night he gets robbed or busted. The only thing is, he doesn't know that's what he's asking himself, so he's always kidding around, asking things like: *When did we become the bad guys?* Or saying stuff like: *Can you believe that when I was a kid I actually wanted to be a cop?*

I had to, he says, finally. She was so proud of me for being on my own, for not having to ask for money. And she had just made one year being sober, I didn't want her to worry. Still, I had to pay the rent... I mean, *you* should understand *that*.

And whenever he gets like this, he always brings it back to me. For the first year, I'd given him hell about it, selling coke. As I said, I had made that mistake. Then, next thing I know, I'm out of school, the restaurant I'm working for shuts down, and I'm staring down the business end of student loans and rent like a revolver. Not to mention the back child support I owe my baby's mama. Close to 1200 bucks.

Listen, I say, finally. This shit is not forever. Neither one of us are confused about that – but for tonight, we've got three very fine looking women following us home to buy cocaine and hang out with us, so let's try to make the best of it.

What's the worst thing you've ever done? he says.

Forget it, man.

No, really.

...and I realize I could say a number of things here...

There was fucking my ex-girlfriend's best friend while my ex-girlfriend was in jail. There was the time I got drunk, cursed at my 90 year-old grandfather on Christmas Eve for waving his empty water glass at the waiter. I once nudged a rent-a-cop out of the way with the bumper of my car after he was trying to pull me and some friends over for doing doughnuts in an empty parking lot one night. More appropriate for the moment, I stole small amounts of cocaine off my roommate and best friend for a year without him knowing it.

The thing is, I was a decent guy once. It didn't get me anywhere. I had a nice girlfriend, I always had a job. I got straight A's, even in college (though I was 22 before I would finally go back to school). I remembered my daughter's birthday, I saved up for Mother's Day gifts. Not only responsible, though, I was cool. I was the guy you called when you needed to be bailed out for drunk driving at 3 am. I'd come out, drunk myself, post bail, and tell you to get me the money when you could.

Then, there was the night I got a flat tire at 1:30 am on a quiet Saturday night/Sunday morning a few years back. Not a week before, I had loaned my spare tire to a friend who drove the same car as me and who'd lost his spare. I called everyone I knew, but no one picked up the phone. I walked a mile or so back to a gas station for a can of Fix-a-flat, but it didn't fix the tire. I tried calling people again – my girlfriend at the time, my best friend, my mom even. But no one answered. The next day, everyone had reasonable excuses. They didn't hear their phone, whatever. I wasn't mad at anybody, it was my own fault. But on the long walk home, I had a thought that if I had been able to call myself, I would have answered.

It was the funniest thing in the world to me, *and I laughed all the way home*

6.

Shit! He tried to bite me!

He's hurt, my roommate says.

I know, I'm trying to help!

All he knows is that a minute ago we hit him with a car...

It's not like we meant to.

Tell him.

I'm gonna try again... Fuck!

Did he get you?

Yeah. Shit! I'm bleeding.

What are you doing now?

I'm letting him smell me. If he won't let me near him, how do we get him to your sister's vet?

Looks like you're putting your hand out so he can bite you easier.

No, I saw this on TV once. Now, shut up, you're making him nervous.

What kind of dog is that anyway?

I don't know... a shaggy one.

Watch out, I think he growled.

That wasn't a growl. He's breathing.

Why's he breathing like that?

All right, I'm going to pick him up. Back the car over here.

He jogs over to the car, backs it to where the dog is lying. As I maneuver my hands under the dog to pick it up, it snaps at my face.

Open the passenger door! You're going to have to drive.

Shit, dude, he says. Your face. He get you again?

Yeah... you know how to get there?

Where?

7.

The twelve Sunday beers in our fridge at the house go pretty quick, but it's cool: Ahmad at the Texaco on Boulevard will sell us beer for cash if I don't make him break a twenty. Yes, children, in those days there were still the blue laws in the south which honored the commandment that you either bought all the booze you needed for Sunday the day before, or else turned water into wine.

Besides, it was starting to look like more beer may not be necessary. I had brought out the bag of cocaine, a full ounce, from the safe in my roommate's room. It was stupid, but I thought it was impressive. Then, I make this bad joke – easy pickings about doing lines of coke off of hookers' backs or something – and before I know it, the brunette is giggling, stretched out across my lap, letting me parse out lines with a credit card on the small of her back. I'm being careful, trying not to scrape her oh-so-soft skin, when she asks how she's going to get hers.

I'll lie across your lap when we're done, I kid her.

And do I get to choose the body part?

The unbelievable part is, she's a kindergarten teacher or some shit. At least that's what she told us. The blonde is in banking or finances or something I know nothing about, and the redhead is a pharmacist. That's as far as the small talk has gotten us.

Across the room, the blonde's sitting with my roommate on the small couch. The blonde keeps trying to flirt with him, saying things to him like, Wow, that's the most cocaine I've ever seen at once.

He's in a drunken trance, though.

The redhead could care less about the whole thing. She keeps saying things to us phrased as compliments, but that might also be condescending. What's more, she won't sit. She just stands, occasionally moving from one side of the room to the other.

I loved that band in college, she says, looking up at the Nine Inch Nails poster behind us on the couch. I think it's cool you guys still have band posters on your walls.

I pick up a bump with the edge of a credit card and reach around slowly, offering it to the brunette. She takes it. Then, I invite the redhead over to do her line. I offer her a rolled up bill, but she shakes her head and pulls an inch of clipped, pink drinking straw from her jeans pocket.

Gotta watch out for Hep C, she says, shrugs, and does her line off the brunette's back.

The blonde takes the bill though, and asks me to hold her hair back. I do, brushing my thumb along her neck. She looks me in the eye and winks.

Don't forget your numbie, I tell her, nodding to the bit left behind.

Thanks, she says, slowly licking the bits of white powder left on the brunette's back.

Hey, what are you guys doing back there? the brunette laughs.

Gettin' my numbie, the blonde says.

I want one! You guys need to share!

All right, the blonde says. And with that, she leans over and sticks out her tongue, touches it to the brunette's.

8.

The parking lot of the vet is empty except for a car that looks like it might have been sitting there for a while.

It looks pretty dark, man.

Drive around to the back. Maybe there's someone on call, sleeping or something.

Looks like an alley back here. No windows...

That metal door. Let's try that.

He gets out, goes over to the door, bangs on it three times.

No one's coming, man! I don't think anyone's here!

Fuck it... keep banging!

9.

The brunette gets up, straightening her top as the perfect image of her arched back and the thin line of her waist gets seared into my memory. I still have that image in my mind to this day, boys, when the nights are cold and long, and my thoughts can't help but turn to sin. She grins, seeing me watching her.

My turn, she says.

All right, but I need to break for just a sec.

I stand up from the couch, and she frowns playfully. My head is spinning.

No fair! she frowns.

I have to take a leak, I say. I'll be back. Patience is a virtue.

Fine, but I want a big, fat one...

I pause, about to say something, then realize there's nothing I can say that wouldn't come off creepy, so I leave it alone. I look over at my roommate, still in his trance. The blonde's got her hand on his thigh.

I never knew drug dealers could be such nice guys, she says.

Yeah, the redhead says, sarcastically. It wasn't like this at all on the after school specials.

I find myself wanting to ask her to sit down, but I'm wondering about all the school references. That's when my roommate perks up.

Nice guys? he slurs. You want to know *the worst thing* I've ever done?

10.

He comes back to the car, gets back in the driver's side.

No one's there, he says, then: Shit. There's got to be someone!

Why? Look, man, I don't think there are emergency vets.

What if someone's dog gets sick in the middle of the night?

They wait until morning. It's a dog!

I can't believe that – some people are nuts about their dogs.

Even still, there's no one here.

So what do we do, wait until morning?

The dog starts whimpering again.

That dog's not going to make it until morning, he says.

What are you talking about?

It's in pain, man. Its breath is all shallow and shit. It's probably bleeding internally. It sounds like one of its lungs is collapsed.

Thanks for the diagnosis. How long have you been in veterinary school?

Look, I'm not saying I know.

So what are you saying?

I'm saying that dog is dying, and it's in a lot of pain. We're talking about doing what's best for him, right?

What are you saying?

I'm saying we got to put him down.

Put him down?

Yeah, you know... put him out of his misery.

I know what it means! What I don't know about is you, you sick, dog-killing fuck!

11.

What the fuck are you *doing*? I say, and in my head, it's to my roommate, but I'm standing in front of the mirror mounted on the medicine cabinet over the sink. I've just finished pissing, and as I'm snorting some water from the faucet up my nose to clear my sinuses, I see my reflection.

I shake my head, splash water on my face.

When I left, my roommate was regaling our guests with talk about the dualism of good and bad and how that is actually what leads to suffering. *Karma*, he says, But not the way most people think about it. *There's no truth or lies, only what is. What should be is the only lie.*

What? I say. Lenny Bruce again?

He went deep brother, you know that. People think you earn karma – but no, it's more like the sum total of the things you'll do and have done rather than what you're doing. People look at it, like it's good or bad, whatever – like, uh, what do you call it? Self-prophecy?

Self-fulfilling prophecy? the redhead asked, rolling her eyes.

Yeah, man, yeah, that's it! he said, then pointing to me: Exactly! What's it called? *Chekhov's gun!*

Do you guys have every Scorsese movie ever made? the redhead said, studying the shelf over the television.

I'm wishing she would sit down.

Ooo! said the blonde. Put on Scarface!

I'm pissing, I said, finally left the room and came into the bathroom to hide out.

Collect myself...

As I'm toweling off my face from the water, the bathroom door opens. It's the brunette, and she's holding the big bag of cocaine from the coffee table, along with her purse slung over her shoulder, like she's afraid to leave her things lying around.

My turn yet?

Jesus, I say, annoyed. Remember what we talked about – patience being a virtue?

I know, she frowns. But it's never been one of mine.

She pulls me to her. She opens her mouth, and I slide my tongue in. Her hand slides down to my crotch.

Now... What body part do *I* choose?

I'm guessing you're not interested in the small of my back.

12.

C'mon man, we did everything we can! We can't just leave it in pain.

We can try another vet, I say, not believing it's me saying it.

Where is there another vet? Tell me.

...I don't know. We go back to the house, google it.

You think he's got time for that? C'mon man, this is the only way...

He looks at me, eyes sad, pleading, and I know, he thinks this is somehow his shot at redemption. All he has to do is do right by this dog. But kill it? We've got to be out of our minds.

Bro... he says, and the dog coughs, sputters.

I look back at him. I try to remember the dog I had until I was 12, as if something about my life up until now had prepared me for this moment. But it was my parent's dog, really, and it was never hit by a car. So instead, the recent rash of life decisions that led me to be standing over the wounded body of a strange dog, drunk and coked up, flashed through my brain. Maybe he's right, I tell myself. Maybe he knows best.

How do we do it? I say.

Do we shoot him?

Man, I don't have a gun! Do you?

No... we got rid of it, remember?

You say that like it's a bad thing.

We'll have to find something to hit it with.

You want to beat it to death? That's real humane!

No, no. One time to the head.

Oh, fuck no!

We got to. Let's look in the trunk.

He hits the latch, the trunk pops.

13.

In my bedroom, I find a key and give the brunette a bump in each nostril to tide her over. I do one myself as she's unbuckling my belt. I drop the bag on the nightstand, pull her to me and kiss her. Then, I pull her shirt over her head and push her back on the bed. She's wearing a black bra that pushes up her full, tan breasts.

I pull off my shirt, lay over top of her. I'm kissing her, when she stops me.

What?

Your bed, she says. Is there something under the mattress?

Move to the center, I tell her. It's just old, lumpy.

I start kissing her neck and breasts, and as I'm reaching for the clasp on her bra, she rolls me over on my back. She reaches off the side of the bed for her purse, brings out a pair of handcuffs. My stomach rushes for my bowels, then it registers that she hasn't pulled out a badge.

I'm feeling pretty stupid, but she hasn't noticed anything.

She stretches my arms back and fits the cuff around one of my hands, when through the half-open bedroom door, I hear the blonde coming down the hall.

Guys? she says, and I'm thinking: *Fuck!*

She peaks in through the door, and the brunette and I look over.

Oh, she says. I'm not interrupting, am I?

No, the brunette says, moving off of me. We were just about to do a line.

I clap my hand to my face, whacking myself with the cuffs in the eye.

Ow, fuck!

Oh baby, the brunette says, trying not laugh. Are you okay?

Fine, fine, I say, rubbing the bridge of my nose and my eye.

Are you sure? the blonde says. That I'm not interrupting?

Of course not, darling, come here...

I take my hands from my face as the blonde gets to the bed, just in time to see them kiss. I sit up, but the brunette pushes me in the chest, and I fall back on the bed.

You can help me choose the body part we do it off, she tells the blonde.

Oh, that sounds like fun.

The blonde lies across the bed a few feet from us as the brunette straddles me.

Is there anymore beer, though? the blonde says. I think our friend needs a beer if she's going to keep hanging out with that guy.

The brunette shoots her a dirty look. The blonde looks back at her, and I can tell these are the residuals of some previous argument I've not been privileged to.

No more beer, I say, remembering grabbing the last two from the fridge a half hour ago. I point to my closet. There's a bottle of bourbon in the floor of my closet, I say. Pretty good stuff.

No, she won't do dark liquor, the blonde says.

She'll be fine, the brunette says. He'll pass out any minute... give him a bourbon. She looks at me, bites her lip and shrugs.

The blonde sits there, contemplating.

Snap that other cuff into place, the brunette says, winks at her.

But I can tell the blonde's not sure.

I sit up.

So let's do a line, I say. Then, we'll run up to the gas station in a while...

No, really. You might need to calm him down first, the blonde says.

Fuck, really?

Really? The brunette shoots her a look, then me, then runs her nails lightly down my chest.

Yeah, he's trying to talk philosophy out there or something.

Did he bring up that 200 hundred bucks he took off his mom?

The blonde nodded.

Fuck.

The brunette sighed.

I stood up, buckled my pants. I found my shirt on the floor and put it on.

I'll ride him up to the store, he'll chill out on the way.

I look back at the bed. The blonde had lay back again and the brunette was leaning over her, twirling her hair.

We'll wait right here, the brunette says.

I really hope so, I say, grinning.

Can we do a bump while you're gone?

I look at the bag on the nightstand, realizing I should probably put it away in the safe.

Sure, I say. Why not?

See, the blonde was saying to the brunette as I was leaving. I told you... nice guys.

14.

A minute later, he comes back from rifling in his trunk.

I found this.

A hammer?

He shrugs.

We can't kill a dog with a hammer!

For chrissakes, man! We got to! Listen to him!

The dog is wheezing, crying out when it tries to breathe deeper.

Fuck. Come open my door, so I can get him out.

He reaches across me, opens the passenger door. Around back of the car, the trunk is open. There's an old pink quilt in it.

Grab that blanket – spread it on the ground.

What for?

To put down, so he's more comfortable. Also, we'll need to cover him up afterwards. You know... to be respectful.

He spreads the blanket out behind the car.

Aaaarff!

Need help getting him down?

Easy, boy... easy. I got it...

I put the dog on the blanket, ease its head on the ground. We're still for a minute, listening to it panting.

So who's going to do it?

We look at each other.

It's my idea, I'll do it.

He stands there for a moment, looking at the hammer in his hand. Then he looks at the dog.

Fuck it, I hit him, I say. He's my responsibility. Give it here...

He hands the hammer over.

15.

I come out to the living room to collect my roommate, and he and the redhead are kissing on the small couch. I'm thinking, *Fuck yes!* And I'm about to turn around and head back to my room when the redhead shoves him off of her. She sits up and smacks him hard across the face. He reels back, falls off the couch.

Motherfucker! she shouts, then turns to me. Tell those bitches there is no fucking way! When's the last time he showered?

Hey, hey, I say, going over, helping him up.

I was just explaining karma, he slurs. How there's no good or bad people, just people. In nature, equiliborum... I mean, equilibrium is reached in the meeting of two opposing forces, right?

I looked at him, and then at the redhead, shaking her head back and forth.

Dude, I say. What the fuck are you talking about?

I was saying how most people are always thinking about karma like it's destiny or fate... like it's good or bad based on whether you're good or bad... but there *is* no good or bad!

I look at him.

He smells so bad, the redhead was saying.

Everything happens for a reason, he rambles. But there's no end to it... it all evens out in the end, right? So what's the point in trying?

Right... I look at the redhead, say: I'm thinking I'm going to ride us up to the gas station to get a 12 pack. You want a beer?

I want to leave, she says, standing up.

Listen, sit down, I tell her. He's just been through a rough time lately. Let us go buy you a beer, and when we get back, he'll be all chilled out. He's not a bad guy really, I say.

That's my point, he says. I'm not a bad guy, you're not a bad guy – there are no *bad* guys, just *guys*.

But I wanted to hang out with you, she says, stepping closer to me. Tell *her* to come out and babysit.

I nod, wondering at the sea change, then I look down the hall, try not to think about what I am missing. I look back to the redhead, who goes up on tiptoes and kisses me on the cheek.

Bring me a beer first? she says, pouting, and not for the first time I'm turned off by how fake it all is. The pageantry of hooking up, of sex, drugs, and rock'n'roll, or whatever.

Let's go get some beer, I say to my friend.

Greatsh... I could use ah drink. I'll drive.

Hell, no, I tell him.

We leave the redhead standing in the living room, find the Sebring parked crooked along the curb out front of the house. I still have the brunette's handcuff around my wrist. I lock the other cuff around the same wrist so it's not dangling and pull my sleeve over it the best I can.

Fortunately, it's less than a mile to the gas station.

What the fuck is wrong with you tonight? I say, pulling out of the neighborhood. The blonde was all over you, and you ignored her. She's cool, she's in finance or something. She's probably loaded. You could be a kept man!

I don't know, he says, suddenly sounding almost sober. Then, he says: You think those girls are okay alone in our place?

What are they going do? I say.

You probably should have taken the coke, man.

What?

I didn't want to tell you, but that's our rent money.

What?

I had to use the rent to re-up after we went to Florida and did all that shit down there on vacation.

What the *fuck*? You said there was plenty in the bank! You were supposed to get a money order and give it to Bob for the rent.

Bob's cool.

He's our landlord! He's cool when we pay the rent!

Look, he says. I didn't want to worry you. You seem like you got enough on your mind lately.

Me? I've got a lot on my, no fucking way... I knew I shouldn't have let you convince me to go on Spring Break.

You needed it though, brother...

We're not even in fucking college!

I'm sorry, man. I am. I thought we needed to get away, and I figured we'd make the money back in no time. I thought we needed a vacation...

Our fucking life is a vacation! *Jesus.*

It's all right, bro. They don't seem like the type to try anything. Besides, we'll be right back.

Yeah.

The kindergarten teacher was the only one who seemed to want it too much.

What? I say, looking at him. Want *what* too much?

Forget it. They're cool – I'm sorry I brought it up in the first place. Besides, I feel like that one girl gets me.

The blonde?

No, the pharmacist. The redhead...

That's when I see something dart into the road.

I slam on the brakes, but it's too late. *There's a thud, punctuated by the sound of screeching tires*

16.

*Stop! G*d, stop!*

I freeze, hammer raised over my head, my other hand on the dog for better aim. I look over towards the metal door, and there's a woman in scrubs running across the parking lot.

What are you doing? What *the hell* are you doing?

Holy shit! Are you a vet? he asks.

I fall back on my ass, hammer in hand. My eyes go blurry, tears start rolling down my cheeks. I put my head between my knees, and before I know it, I'm bawling.

We banged for half an hour, I hear him explaining.

The doorbell, she says. The button to the right of the door... with the sign.

Sign?

The one that says: RING IN CASE OF EMERGENCY.

Oh, man.

Is he okay? she says, and I'm not sure if she's talking about me or the dog.

The woman in scrubs is close to our age. She has a nose ring and tattoos, but at the same time, she carries herself like someone who had never drank too much and did too much coke and gone out driving. I take deep breaths. I bring my arm up to wipe my face with my sleeve, but a little too quickly – I end up knocking myself in the face with the handcuffs in the same spot I had earlier.

Mother-fuck, I say. Mother-fuck!

She's the vet tech, this woman, and when I get it together enough to pick up the dog again, she leads us inside. We walk through a room with dogs and cats in kennels. From there, we go through a door to an examination room where she tells me to put the dog down on a metal table. As I back away, keeping my hand on the dog to steady it, the tech is looking at the handcuffs around my wrist, and I shrug.

Long story, I tell her. I promise I'm not on the lam.

She just stands there, looking at me.

From the cops, anyway, I say, try to grin.

What kind of dog is that? my buddy asks. It's so shaggy...

But the veterinarian comes in, and we stay with them until they inject the dog with painkillers. Then, we go back outside, and my roommate lights a cigarette. After taking a few puffs, he hands it over, and I take a long drag.

After a few minutes, the vet tech comes back outside. She asks for a smoke. My buddy hands her the pack, then the lighter.

He ran out in front of us, I tell her. I couldn't... We didn't want it to suffer.

She holds up the hand with the smoke in it.

It's okay, she says. Most people wouldn't have stopped.

It sounds forced though, like she's still trying to figure out what to do with us there, two attempted dog murderers, haggard and mad on the doorstep of her workplace.

After we finish the cigarette, we go back inside. The vet tech looks at the places where the dog bit me. She rubs them with alcohol and tells me it's a good idea to get a tetanus shot. Then, I have to fill out some papers saying I will be responsible if they can't find the owner.

I look at her, then at my friend.

He shrugs.

We'll find where she lives, the tech says. She's got the collar.

She?

Yeah, it's a girl.

No wonder she bit you, my roommate says. All that *good boy* stuff.

I'm staring at the wall at a poster about heartworms, wondering how the fuck I ended up there when the vet tech pats me on the shoulder.

Most people wouldn't have stopped, she says again.

She means it this time, or wants to, I can tell – but I'm not sure how it should make me feel. It seems like she's decided I'm not such a bad guy after all. Still, if I am honest with myself, I'm not really sure I deserve that designation.

As we pull out of the parking lot, the first stoplight we come to is red. Exhausted, I want to run it, but don't. I remember *the blonde, the brunette, and the redhead* The financier, the kindergarten teacher, and the pharmacist. I am trying to remember their names, but my brain feels like someone bored a couple of holes through it.

You know, she's right, he says. Most guys would've just left her there.

I don't answer.

I was thinking... maybe this is a sign or something.

In my experience, signs are usually a little more subtle.

You know... he says. My mom doesn't live far away.

Finally, the light changes.

It's still an hour before she gets up to go to work, he says. Maybe I could sneak in, leave 200 bucks on her dresser.

I start to ask him if we might need that for rent, but I'm too tired.

The billboards and the city skyline were just out the window, cruising alongside us as we turned on Freedom Parkway. It looked so dramatic, the city in the dawn, and I felt a twinge in the pit of my stomach. I don't know what it is, but any city at that time of day gives me that feeling.

We drive a mile or so down the road, past where we would have turned to go back, then turn off into a neighborhood. We cut through a labyrinth of residential streets, winding, cutting across larger cross streets back into more residential ones. Finally, he tells me to stop in a cul de sac.

He opens the car door, looks at me.

I shrug.

He's inside for a long time. Finally, the car door opens, and I wake. The day is getting bright, and it hurts my eyes. I can feel a bitch of a headache coming on.

So?

She was awake.

Shit... So what'd you do?

I gave her the money.

Yeah?

Yeah.

What'd she say?

She just asked if I had been drinking.

What'd you tell her?

I told her I had.

And?

And she made me a cup of coffee.

I pull out of the driveway. We make our way back through the neighborhoods and through town. When we get back to our house, the sun is fully up, and it's a beautiful day. I can hardly wait to shut the blinds, get in bed, and sleep through it.

The blonde, the brunette, and the redhead are long gone. The banker, the kindergarten teacher, the pharmacist. *What kind of professionals go home with a couple of cocaine dealers the night before Easter Sunday, anyway?* I ask myself.

I go straight into my room and fall on the bed, the side nearest the door. It's lumpy near the head, and I remember I hid my roommate's revolver underneath the mattress after I made him give it to me a couple of weeks back. What else was I supposed to do with it? Leave it lying around for a kid to find? I figured at some point I'd dump it in a lake or down a storm drain like I'd seen on *The Wire*, but I hadn't gotten around to it.

I close my eyes, see the arch of the brunette's back followed by the thin line of her waist as it disappeared under her top, remember the cocaine. I open my eyes, look over at the nightstand, but I already know it's not there. I clap my hand to my face, knock myself in the forehead one last time with the handcuffs. I think about going in the other room to tell him, but I don't.

Let him sleep, I tell myself. After all, *there is no should be, only what is.* What is, which looks to be a couple of assholes. So I lay there, listening to my head throb with hangover and self-loathing, a rim shot repeating around my brain.

INSTANT GLAMOR

It was 2 am, and Lisa was taking Marti home after meeting a john at a hotel across town. She had driven for Marti many times, and it was always easy money – no worries. Marti was one of the two or three girls Lisa drove for, and she liked her, because Marti was smart about it. She refused to meet johns in bad places, and she never went with random guys. Tonight, for instance, the date had run late, and Marti was slow to call down, but it had been a nice hotel and a classy guy so there wasn't much cause for worry. Now, there was just the ride home, and Lisa was listening to Marti talk about Bruce – one of her regulars – a recently divorced club owner who wanted her to quit turning tricks and marry him.

He's handsome in his way, Marti said. Big. I like big guys. But he needs a woman around – he has this awful toupee he wears – he needs someone to tell him. When will these poor guys learn to just shave it? Lisa kept her eyes on the road. *But*, he's nice to me, and he's got money enough to take care of a girl.

Unlike the other girls Lisa drove for, Marti was more talkative on the rides back. She was in her mid-thirties, though she looked somewhat older. There were lines under her eyes – thin, deep creases. But she had an established clientele. She took on fewer new clients each year because she had a customer base of men who talked about marrying her one day, men that gave her expensive clothes and jewelry. Bruce, though in his sixties, was a leading contender.

You think everything's forever when you're young, she said, then laughed. At least I did. Never thought about a retirement plan. But this work is tough on a girl after a while. She pulled the visor down, checked her make-up in the mirror, closed it. I want to tell your friend about it, she said. Heidi. She needs to think down the road some – not spend it all on new clothes and coke – but she wouldn't hear it. Not right now.

Heidi, who Lisa met taking summer classes at the community college, was the girl who got her started driving for hookers. Working girls liked to have someone waiting on them, someone who knew to call somebody if they weren't out by a certain time. Heidi had worked as a waitress at a strip club, which was how she knew the girls who turned tricks. In the two years Lisa knew her, Heidi had gone from waitressing to stripping, from driving to turning tricks herself.

You, though, *babe – you're* smart, Marti said. Still in school. You're a *good girl.*

Not that good, Lisa said, but it stuck in her throat.

Lisa was set to graduate at the end of the semester with a master's in public health. She started driving girls to meet their johns the summer after she graduated with her bachelor's, and soon quit her job waiting tables. It was easy money, and what's more, there was a certain allure in the proximity to danger – a rough glitter that made her think of asphalt. It often gave her a little bit of a rush.

Proximity to danger was something Lisa had craved ever since her mother had died, shortly before she graduated high school. It was only proximity though, she was careful not to let herself go too far. While Heidi eventually started turning tricks, Lisa had been driving working girls for a year and a half now, and hadn't given into the temptation.

It was not that she couldn't imagine herself doing it. It *was* great money, and she felt like she could detach her body enough from her experience that she wouldn't feel scarred after. It was mainly that she never felt glamorous enough.

Implants, Heidi had said, when Lisa told her this. *Instant glamour.*

But it depressed Lisa to remember her friend's perfect B-cup and to think of the insanity of a culture that would have made that inadequate. It was that aspect that made her feel distant from it. Otherwise, the idea of prostitution didn't really bother her. Sure, it was easy to cry foul for women enslaved into it – junior year, she had interned in the U.S. office of a nonprofit that sheltered these women – but for women born here, it was a choice. At least as much as anything in life was.

They were on their way back to Marti's apartment building in Midtown when Lisa hit something small in the road. She slowed, not seeing what it was, and she didn't really think about it until the car started getting resistance from behind, and there was a loud thumping.

You're gonna have to pull over, honey, Marti said. You got a flat.

Lisa slowed down, pulled off to the side of the road, then saw a street maybe twenty yards ahead. She drove the extra distance slowly, turned off on the side street. She got out, surveyed the tire on the back driver's side, not entirely sure what she was looking for. This was the first time she had a flat. Lisa looked around. They were on North, but it was a residential stretch, and early morning besides, so there were no other cars in sight.

Marti got out and came around. It was October, and the nights were getting cooler. She zipped up the dark blue hoodie she wore over her short, black evening dress.

She had a collection of furs and leather coats that she wore between the car and the john, but she would usually trade them out when she got back to the car. It was a trick she learned to not look like a prostitute if pulled over, to keep from getting harassed by cops and getting her cash stolen.

She took out a pack of Newports, lit a cigarette. She stood smoking, watching the girl crouching to survey the tire. After a minute, Lisa stood, walked around to the trunk and opened it. She pulled out the jack and the ratchet and came back and laid them out on the asphalt next to the tire. She stood over them.

You've never changed a tire before, have you? Marti said.

Lisa shrugged, embarrassed. Not only could she not change a flat, she had never had one, and she hadn't known for sure what was happening, not until Marti told her to pull over.

We could call Triple A, she said. I'm on my Dad's membership.

Marti laughed. She took a drag of her Newport 100. All the girls smoked 100s – they were more *elegant*.

First, Marti said. You need to get the spare out. They keep them screwed down tight in the trunk, and you don't want to be trying to get it out with your car balanced on a jack...

Lisa nodded, went back to the trunk, and unscrewed the tire. She hefted it from the trunk, and Marti held the cigarette out as Lisa rolled the tire back around. She balanced it against the flat tire, took the cigarette, dragged on it, and handed it back to Marti.

She couldn't help being impressed as Marti started rattling off directions. She had known Marti to be such a girl's girl – she was Martinique to her clients – and she was always complaining about chipping her nails, which she religiously had manicured every time she met a john. Marti explained to first loosen the bolts, then described the notch where the jack fit the frame of the car. Then, she told her how to fit the spare on, and replace the bolts, the whole time looking out at the deserted street, chain-smoking.

It took about half an hour to change the flat. Lisa was sweating, tired in her muscles, as she finally tightened down the bolts of the spare.

And that's that, Marti said, as Lisa stood to use her foot on the ratchet. You just changed a tire.

Just then, a squad car passed. The blue tops flashed briefly as it cut a U in the middle of North, pulled into the side street behind them. Lisa held her breath, hoped Marti was clean. She knew the woman to be a sometimes speed junkie and to dabble in coke – though she seemed sober enough that night. A patrolman – maybe in his forties, tall and hefty in the middle – got out of the roller. He lumbered up to them.

You ladies having a problem? he said, shining his flashlight in their faces, then over their bodies. He cut it off.

No, officer, Marti answered. Problem solved.

He grinned, his teeth white in the amber light of the streetlamp above, the rest of his face a shadow under the brim of his patrolman's cap.

You don't need a ride somewhere? he said. Don't want a DUI now.

No sir, officer, Marti said, slow and easy. It was a voice that had dealt with cops before. She was playing with the zipper of her hoodie, zipping it down past the neck of her low-cut dress, then slightly back up. Nothing like that. We just had a flat on the way home from the Waffle House. We got it sorted out.

Never a cop around when you need one, he said.

Marti laughed. He handed her his card.

You could change that.

I'll keep that in mind, she told him.

You girls *be safe*, he said, turning back to the patrol car.

Lisa cringed. She had always hated that phrase – the way it implied that life could be lived absent any risk. She always preferred *take care* – a phrase her mother used – as it seemed to acknowledge that danger was inherent in anything and only that a person should be mindful of it.

Surely, officer, Marti said, then under her breath: *Pig.*

The cop sat in the patrol car, waited as they got in their car and turned around. He waved as they passed back by him turning onto North. In the rearview, Lisa saw him back out onto North in their direction. He followed them at a distance for maybe quarter of a mile. He caught up with them when Lisa made a last minute decision to stop at a traffic light as it turned yellow.

Breathe, honey, Marti said. He's just showing us what a big guy he is.

Lisa realized that she was holding her breath. She hadn't known Marti knew he was behind them, felt relieved that she had noticed.

Finally, the light turned green. Lisa accelerated slowly through the intersection, watching him in the rearview the whole time. The cop did not move at first, but once she was through the light, he cut another sharp U turn and drove off the way he had come.

They were quiet the rest of the way back to Marti's apartment. She lived in an old three-story brick building on Charles Allen. There was a drive going down around back to a side door and off-street parking. Across the drive was the building's twin, making the drive into an alley. Sitting in the car, between the buildings, Marti gave Lisa a cigarette from her pack, then passed her a thin roll of bills.

There's fifty too much, Lisa said.

There's always more when police are involved –
even if it's nothing.

Lisa nodded.

He didn't scare you, did he? We were fine, y'know.

I know, she said. I was feeling bad about the tire,
actually.

What? Marti joked. Thought I was the kind of girl
who couldn't change a flat?

 It's more that I thought of myself as the kind of a
girl who could...

It's okay, Marti said. Besides, now you know, right?

Yeah, I guess, it's just – She paused. I was always a
tomboy, y'know?

Daddy's girl, huh?

Yeah... Lisa said, but her voice cracked, broke as the
word trailed off.

Believe it or not, babe, I was too.

Lisa cleared her throat. Then, senior year in high
school, she said. My mom gets sick... cancer.

Awful. She didn't make it?

The doctors gave her two years with chemo, but she
researched what it would do, refused it. She took one last
drag from the cigarette, threw it out the window. She died
after six months.

That doesn't give a girl a long time. You have to get
used to the idea of life without a mother. Lot of things need
sorting out, forgiving. 'Specially at that age.

Lisa swallowed.

Anyway, she said. My dad treated me like I was fragile after – has ever since.

Afraid of losing his other girl, I bet. Marti was smiling sadly, her eyes soft. She was looking through the dark into Lisa's eyes. Lisa felt her own face, expressionless. Marti reached over, ran her fingers through Lisa's hair. It was pulled back, but she pulled lightly at the stray hairs around the ear, brushed them back.

Come inside, Marti said, stroking the girl's cheek. I could use some company. I'm always wired after a trick.

Lisa turned her head. Marti's hand hung in air for an instant, then she let it down onto the center console of the car.

I – Lisa started. I need to get home... get cleaned up.

I can run you a bath, Marti said. I have some wine.

Lisa didn't answer.

Or I could make tea...

I can't... not tonight.

I understand. Class tomorrow?

Yeah, Lisa said, though it was Friday, and Fridays she was off.

Marti smiled.

You have such lovely blue eyes, she said. Even in the dark, you can tell how blue they are. They remind me of my little girl. Eyes like her daddy.

She opened the car door, and the dome light came on. Under the dome light, Lisa saw the lines in Marti's face. The crow's feet and creases in her forehead were apparent.

I didn't know you had a daughter, Lisa said.

She doesn't live with me. She's been with my sister going on four years.

Lisa didn't know what to say.

She's going to be seven in November. Wait, no, eight... Jesus.

Marti turned, pulled herself out of the car. She groaned.

This business is hard on the body, she said. Nobody ever tells you that.

She dug in her purse, found her cigarettes again. She lit one, then closed the car door. She started walking down the drive, towards the side door of the building.

Lisa wondered if she misjudged the situation. She knew that Marti had been in relationships with women – a lot of the girls she drove for preferred women after the way they had been treated by men they serviced – that Marti was one had made her nervous. She did like Marti, felt bad that the only way out for her seemed to be to marry a former john. She wondered if there shouldn't be a retirement plan for hookers.

As she turned to back out of the drive way, she looked, saw Marti's fur in the backseat. She rolled the car window down, called her name.

Marti turned, and Lisa rolled down the drive to meet her.

Your coat, she said, out the window.

Oh, rats! Marti said. She took the fur through the open window.

Lisa was taken aback by the expression. It seemed too quaint.

Marti, Lisa said.   Marti bent down to lean her head in the window.   Thanks... for showing me how to change a tire.

Sure thing, kiddo, she said. Take care, now.

MERIDIAN

She didn't wake up at the first exit – she slept right through pulling off and turning around in the dark Texaco parking lot and getting back on the interstate. She shifted once on the exit ramp, and I thought she might wake up, but she only adjusted the jacket folded under her head for a pillow. She had slept for the last couple of hours, most of the way through Alabama and over the Mississippi line and through Meridian. She finally woke up when I pulled off at the next exit, which was a good distance down the road. She sat up, brushed her light brown bangs back from her eyes. She had been wearing her hair up, but it had fallen down while she was sleeping.

She pulled the vanity mirror down to fix her hair as I made the turn off the exit. There was a BP right there in the parking lot of a Save-Rite, but the station was closed. It was after two in the morning.

Where are we? she asked, rubbing her eyes.

Somewhere in Mississippi.

Wow, I slept for a while.

Yeah, you did. Feeling better?

Mmm-hmm. We need gas? Good, I have to pee.

Yeah, but it looks like this place is closed.

The sign on the ramp had said there was another gas station a mile and a half to the left – an Exxon. I told her that and asked if she thought we should go to the next exit or try down the road.

That one could be closed too, she said. We might as well keep making time.

I was trying to be overly agreeable to her. We were on I-59 headed to New Orleans to visit my younger brother and to spend New Year's there. He had not come home over Christmas after he and my parents had gotten into it because he told them he was dropping out of Tulane.

She had been in a bad mood all day. She waited tables and had to work the early cut on the Monday night we were leaving. She had tried to get it covered, but no one wanted the shift the day after Christmas. I drove her to work, and the entire way there, she wouldn't let up about it – how she couldn't believe that no one would take her shift after she had covered for practically everyone. I had made a comment about how they probably wanted to spend time with family, and she started in on me, saying they were professional waiters and college students, that they just wanted to get drunk.

Then she started in on Pat, the owner, and how after working for him three years, he wouldn't give her one night off. I had worked for Pat before her and knew him to be a fair guy, but when I told her that, she asked me whose side I was on. So I backed off to let her vent. Getting out of the car, she apologized for being difficult, but by the time I picked her up, it was worse.

It was almost 10:30 at that point, and they had been slammed. To make it worse, I was thirty minutes late because I had stopped by a friend's house to pick up a bag of weed for the trip. As soon as she got in the car, I realized I left my brother's gifts sitting in the office bedroom at home. After an hour on I-20, she still hadn't let up about having to go back for them, and I couldn't take it anymore – I pulled out a joint and lit up.

Could you please not smoke that right now? she said.

What?

Will you please not smoke that in the car with me?

But I thought you might have some, I said, holding in the hit.

No, and you knew I wouldn't too. I haven't in six months.

Yeah, but I figured –

What?

We're on vacation...

You know I'm going to start going for job interviews soon – I might get drug tested. I don't want to be a waiter all my life.

I knew that she had said that for my benefit. At twenty-five, I hadn't gone to college, and I had worked the same job tending bar for the last four years. Even though I made good money, she resented it for some reason. I took another pull on the joint and put it out. I cracked the window to let the smoke out, but she said she was cold, so I rolled it up again and turned the heat up a notch. Ten minutes later, she was warm and cracked the window. Then she was cold again and turned the heat up until it was blistering hot.

Finally, she fell asleep. *It's P.M.S., that's all,* I told myself. At least I hoped it was – she had been late before, and it had always turned out to be nothing in the past.

After she had been asleep for some time, I cracked the window to see if she would wake up. She didn't, so I lit the joint again, and she slept through that, and then through all of Alabama and Meridian and on into Mississippi. She didn't miss much – pine trees and more pine trees. At night, it all looked the same.

In Meridian, I had stopped at an all-night place and got coffee. I had seen the gas down below a quarter of a tank, but I figured it would give us another hour, and by then, she would be awake and wanting to stop, so I decided to wait.

Sometime later, I looked down, and the warning light was on. I clicked the odometer to register the number of miles we'd gone, something I always do on a trip. My car could go fifty miles on the light, maybe a few extra on the highway, but luckily, I saw a sign for gas at the next exit.

That was the Texaco – the first place that was closed. After the second place, which was in the parking lot of a closed supermarket (and having decided not to try the one down the road), we got back on the interstate. As we were driving, we came to a sign that said the next exit was in three miles. I didn't see any of the blue signs for gas or food, so we passed that exit. There was another a few miles later that didn't have anything either. Finally, we passed a sign that said it was the last gas station for nine miles.

Guess we better stop here, I said.

Looks like it.

She still looked sleepy. I pulled off the road and the sign pointed to the right 0.6 miles. I drove until I saw a Texaco, but it was dark. She didn't say anything until we got back on the interstate.

What are we going to do?

It's fine, I said. The light just came on. We've got plenty of time.

Why didn't you get gas when we stopped earlier? she asked.

What?

When we stopped earlier? Why didn't you get it then?

I thought you were asleep.

I woke up when you were inside the diner. There was a gas station right across the street.

I didn't know.

Her tone changed: Well, why didn't we stop there?

I don't know... we just didn't.

Well, we should have.

Well, we fucking didn't.

Well, why the fuck not? Enlighten me as to why we were at a gas station and didn't get gas.

Because! I yelled, finally losing my temper. Because! Because! *Fucking* because!

No – I want to know. How much gas did we have then?

I sped up. I figured the sooner we made the nine miles to the next gas station, the sooner she'd lay off.

Answer me, she said. How much gas did we have then?

We're going to be fine, all right?

Jesus Christ! She threw up her hands. You can't even answer me.

Her voice had trailed off, and she sat back in her seat. She looked out the window and was silent.

I felt like we'd been having this argument for months – not about gas, but always about something stupid. And then she would use the arguments to bring up things about me which pissed her off, like my smoking pot, or poorly managing my money, or whether or not I was ever going back to college. At first, I didn't get it. I couldn't see how I was any different from when we had started dating three years ago. But after a while, I figured out the real issue was that she was just trying to put pressure on me to get married. She had said many times that she wanted to wait until she finished school, and she had been out for three months.

Our mothers had both been dropping hints about the holidays being a good time to get engaged, and over Christmas, I realized I had to ask her soon or not ask her at all. On Christmas Eve, I took her back in the guest bedroom at my parent's house. I sat her on the bed and got down on one knee and everything.

Okay, she said, when I showed her the ring.

At first I got worried because that's all she said, but then she started crying and told me how happy I had always made her. So we kissed and went back to the living room and told our families, who were spending Christmas together for the first time. They were expecting it, obviously, but everybody got to get really excited, and it seemed like a good thing.

But the excitement only lasted for the next day when my family went to her parents' house for Christmas dinner. Afterwards, when we got back to our apartment, we got into it about whose car to take to New Orleans. She was convinced my car was in better shape, even though the transmission was failing. Her car needed tires, but I thought they had enough tread to make the trip. She kept trying to make it about something else though, saying that we were always broke, and that she was worried it wasn't ever going to get any easier. That was when she told me she was two weeks late.

We didn't talk at all between exits. I wanted to smoke the rest of the joint, but that would have set her off again, so I just drove. We passed three or four exits, but there was nothing at any of them. I was going ninety, trying not to watch the gas light emanating from the dash. The rest of the lights were a soft, tranquil green color, but the damn gas light was a panic-stricken orange. I felt like shouting, *Look, I get it already! We're out of gas! Shut the fuck up!* But I knew I was being ridiculous, and finally, I saw a sign for gas again – a BP station.

I pulled off at the exit and went down the ramp. This gas station was in the parking lot of a grocery store also, and I wondered if it was some kind of trend in Mississippi, similar to the one of nothing being open after midnight.

I turned around in the drive, and drove back to the sign at the ramp. There was an Exxon down the road a little way, but I went back to the interstate. I figured we had over twenty miles before we were in trouble, and there had to be an open gas station soon.

Why aren't we stopping?

It was closed.

I know. The sign said there was another station down the road.

The next exit's probably closer.

If you say so.

I kept driving – I was up around ninety-five, trying not to worry when we passed an exit with no signs for anything. I kept thinking: *Fucking backwater state with no all night gas stations...* Then I saw a sign for a Texaco at the next exit that said it was the last one for nine miles again. I wasn't even worried then. Surely, they wouldn't have a stretch of thirty miles with no all-night gas stations. It was ridiculous. It sounded illegal.

I got off the interstate and drove until I saw it.

Fuck!

Another one? she said. Aren't there any open gas stations in this backwater state?

That's when it first occurred to me what was happening. I looked at her out of the corner of my eye as I was getting back on the interstate. She was looking down.

What the fuck? I said, mostly under my breath.

What?

Nothing.

I told myself I was just stoned.

I went ninety-five the whole way to the next exit, telling myself we'd make it. We'd have to. It was just too stupid not to make it at that point. I mean, think about it, to run out of gas in the middle of the night in Mississippi. It was like a bad movie. Where were the psychotic rednecks? Where was the banjo music playing in the background?

You never answered me, she said calmly.

What?

About why we didn't get gas in – what's the name of that place?

Baby, c'mon, I said. We're on vacation. Let's not fight the entire time.

I'm not, she said. I just want to know.

I thought it would be a good excuse to stop down the road. I thought you'd wake up and have to go to the bathroom, and I probably would too after drinking coffee.

Well, I have to go pretty bad.

Me too.

Why didn't we just stop? she sighed. She wasn't really saying it to me as much as she was saying it to the air, but it pissed me off anyway.

Jesus Christ! I said. What do you want?

Nothing, I just have to pee, and I don't want to run out of gas!

Do you want me to pull off here?

Yeah, that'd be fine for you, wouldn't it?

It's not like you've never done it before.

But it sucks when you're a girl. You don't have any toilet paper.

We'll come to a place soon, I said. It'll be all right.

But I wasn't sure at that point. We only had another ten miles or so on the light, and I was beginning to wonder if there were any open gas stations in the entire state.

I just don't understand why there aren't gas stations open past midnight in this fucking state, she said.

I don't know, babe.

And I don't get why you didn't just stop in Meridian.

Christ, let it go!

I held my breath for a ten count. For some reason, it pissed me off even more that she used the name of the place when she didn't know it before.

So how much gas did we have at that point?

I don't know!

You're driving, why don't you know?

A quarter of a tank, all right? We had a quarter of a tank.

A fourth of a tank of gas... and you didn't stop.

I didn't know there would be no open gas stations in the entire state of Mississippi!

It doesn't matter! There was no reason not to fill up!

I just explained my reasoning. It was mainly for you.

No, it wasn't! You were being lazy. You were stoned, and you didn't feel like doing it.

No, I was stoned, and I didn't want you to wake up and start bitching!

Oh, fuck you!

At that point I saw a sign for gas and pulled off. I rolled through the stop at the bottom of the ramp and saw a closed BP in the parking lot of a Save-Rite. I cut a U-Turn in the road and went under the overpass, but instead of getting back on the highway, I went on. The sign on the ramp had said there was another station, an Exxon, down the road. Seeing the sign, I knew, but I didn't want to say anything about it if I didn't have to.

You're going to get us pulled over, she said.

I looked down, saw I was going seventy-five on a two lane.

So fucking what?

So you want a bunch of redneck cops in Mississippi to search your car and find pot?

I slowed down to sixty.

The Exxon station was closed too, so I drove back to the highway. I knew I had to be careful this time, but as we came to the overpass, I was focused on the dash.

How many miles have we gone on the light? she asked.

Almost forty. It was forty-eight.

Back on the highway, I saw a sign for another exit, but when we passed it, there was nothing there. A short time later, we passed another.

What are we going to do? she said.

I don't know. I have no idea.

Well, you got us into this mess.

That's fine – I did. It's my fault entirely, I admitted.

That's when we passed the sign again.

What the fuck? I said.

What? What is it?

The sign said that after the next exit the next gas station is nine miles.

Shit. Now we're screwed.

What the fuck? Don't you see?

What?

It's the same fucking roads.

What?

It's the same fucking roads every time.

I pulled off at the next exit and went under the bridge to the Texaco, still locked up tight.

It's the same one—the same Texaco. And that exit back there, with the BP in the parking lot of the grocery store.

What are you talking about?

It's the same exits, over and over again.

You're stoned!

No, no. Each time, there was an Exxon a mile and a half down the road.

Oh, Jesus – you got stoned, and you put us going the wrong way on the highway. I can't fucking believe it.

Twice? How could I fuck up twice?

Three times, now. It's the only explanation.

It's not much of one! I don't think I'd go the wrong way three times. I was looking for a sign to say whether we were going east or west, but there were no signs at that point.

She lifted her fingers to her lips, puffing an imaginary joint.

Fucking Christ! I'm not even stoned anymore!

I can't believe you did this.

Did this? Did what?

Got us turned around with no gas!

You're insane, I'm not turned around! This is just – I don't know what it is – it's crazy.

I can't believe you did this to us.

I looked over, saw she was crying. I got out of the car and slammed the door. I went behind the Texaco and took a leak in the brush. She was still crying when I returned. Sick of fighting, I put my arm around her and kissed her on the head.

It's fine, I said. Whatever happens, it'll be fine.

What are we going to do?

We'll go on. We've still got some time.

How far can we go on the light?

We still have another few miles, I lied.

Maybe we should just stay here until morning.

Maybe.

But it's so dark out here.

What do you want to do? I said. I got us into this mess.

I don't know, whatever you think.

Let's go on, then. But I don't know why I said it, when I knew we wouldn't even make it back to the closed BP. I guess I decided it was probably what she wanted to do.

What if we don't make it?

But I had already turned around and was headed back to the interstate.

We'll make it. It'll be fine.

I was careful getting on this time, making sure I went west, even though it had to be the other exit where I somehow kept getting turned around.

We're in the middle of nowhere, she said.

We'll make it, I told her. But I couldn't see how.

HAPPILY EVER AFTER

A few minutes before the oven timer went off, she lost it. She threw the Waterford vase his mother had sent for their anniversary at him. She missed his head by three feet, but it smashed into pieces against the wall behind him. She wasn't really trying to hit him, but he was drunk, so there was no way to make him understand that, and they ended up grappling on the new hardwood floors. On the floor, she kneed him in the crotch and freed herself enough to reach the half-empty scotch bottle on the counter. She smashed it over his head.

Bitch! he screamed, reeling. That's alcohol abuse! It was only half-empty!

Half-full! You limp-dick, cynical son of a bitch!

He shoved her through the doorway into the living room. Then he picked her up and threw her over the counter of the wet bar. Getting up, she staggered back into the glass shelves, knocking down rows of bottles and glasses.

He looked across the room at the flat screen TV. The game was on. He checked the score out of habit, but before it registered, she was back at him with a corkscrew. He caught her arms, but her momentum pushed them back into the kitchen. He managed to wrestle the corkscrew away from her, but she slipped on her socked feet, and fell back, hitting her head on the granite countertop. She got up slow, balancing herself on the island in the middle of the kitchen. When he saw her bleeding from her head, he got scared.

Baby... ? He made his way over to her slowly.

When he was in close, she grabbed a paring knife from the wooden cutting board just behind her and stabbed him in the side. He fell back into the stainless steel doors of the refrigerator, slid to the kitchen tiles. Getting up, he pushed his elbow back against the refrigerator door to stand up, and he hit the lever on the ice machine. Some crushed ice fell onto the floor.

The oven timer went off. Holding the knife in his side, he walked out the back door into the cool, summer air. He looked up at the moon, laughed. It was almost full.

When he pulled the knife out, he was dizzy and felt his eyes roll back into his head. He fell through the glass patio table they had bought last summer after one of the worst fights they had ever had. Eventually, she had forgiven him.

Mercury had been in retrograde, she had said, making communication difficult.

He woke up a few minutes later.

Feeling okay, he got to his feet and walked back inside to find her sobbing on the kitchen floor. It was quiet except for the crying. She had turned off the oven timer.

I thought you were dead, she sobbed.

He stood there watching her with his dark eyes, the way he did sometimes. When he did that, his eyes seemed to look through her clothes, exploring every inch of her, every crevice. She smiled. He came over, picked her up off the ground, and carried her into the bedroom. They grappled and tugged at each other until they were naked on the bed, blood soaking the white sheets, 1500 thread count Egyptian cotton. When it was finished – they both made it without the other even having to ask, it was that explosive – they lay across the bed like wet laundry waiting to be hung.

You okay? he asked, feeling a little faint.

She shook her head yes.

You might need stitches for that.

He kissed her head.

What about your side?

It's nothing.

When the blue lights appeared in the window, he sat up in bed. A minute later, there was a knock on the front door. He dressed quickly, she threw on a robe. They went to the door together.

They told the policeman at the door that everything was fine, that they were just making dinner. The policeman eyed them up and down.

You sure? he asked her, raising an eyebrow at the blood-soaked washcloth she held to her temple.

Yes sir, he answered for her.

The policeman looked at him, saw the blood from his side soaking through the t-shirt he had thrown on.

Yes, Officer, she said.

The policeman looked behind them into the house, but he couldn't see much beyond the darkened foyer.

It smells like something's burning.

No sir, he said.

That's just dinner, she said.

Okay, then... You folks have a good night.

Thank you, Officer, they said in unison.

The policeman turned back as he was going down the walk, saw them standing in the doorway together, the man's arm around the woman's shoulders, they were both waving. Something wasn't right, but his shift was almost over. Walking back to his patrol car, he surveyed the neatly manicured lawn, the well-trimmed shrubs, and the seasonal flowers planted in the wood chip islands. He stopped, looked up at the moon. They seemed normal enough. Still, one could only imagine the kinky shit these suburban types were into.

ANY CONSTELLATION

1.

I wish I could say that I didn't see the railroad bridge coming, that I didn't even think about there being a clearance issue, but I did. I was coming down the hill on College – not going too fast, but a little faster than I should have been – headed back to work after stopping off at Ashton's house to help him and some friends kill a keg of beer from the previous night. The speakers of the big, white catering truck were strained, not quite at full blast. I saw the bridge, did some quick estimations, thought that even the though the truck height and the clearance height were the same, they had to leave a few inches just in case. They didn't. There was an awful scraping like the sound of some prehistoric creature dying a painful death, and I smacked my head on the steering wheel. I sat there, dazed, fossilized, under the amber light of the tunnel.

Shit, I said. Shit, shit, shit...

Okay, I told myself. *This isn't necessarily as bad as it seems.*

I put the truck in reverse. *Nothing.* I tapped the gas lightly, still nothing. *Shit.* I got out of the truck, stepped back. *Shit. Shitshitshitshitshitshit...* Was all I could say, for like 10 minutes. Somewhere in the long line of cars slowly going around, a pick-up truck full of rednecks rolled by laughing. One, in a hat with a rebel flag, leaned his head out the window: *Got 'er stuck, did'n ya?*

I stood there a few minutes longer, then went back, got in the truck. I knew the cops would be coming any minute. I tried to breathe. The cops didn't come. Not knowing what else to do, I called Cara on the company cell in the glove compartment, told her I needed her to get out there quick.

Shit, she had said, but that was it.

I had gotten a half-hearted *Where the fuck have you been?* when she picked up, but I knew her well enough to know it wasn't real anger. Then: Don't do anything, I'm on my way. There'd be no lectures. G*d, I loved Cara.

Once she was on the way, I felt brave enough to try again.

I turned the ignition, put it in reverse. Nothing. So I put it in drive. No. Reverse again – a noise in my head like sandpaper on the scalp. But it budged. So I did it again. And again. Forward and back, forward and back, until – the prehistoric creature from before made a final horrifying death rattle that signaled extinction for its entire species – it was free.

2.

The cops still hadn't shown up when Cara got there. *An Easter Eve miracle*, I remember thinking. I watched her pull off onto the shoulder in her five year-old-piece-of-shit Ford Probe. It might have been the fucking Batmobile, though, coming to my rescue, and it was everything I could do to stand and watch her park, get out of the car, and wait for her come to me. As we surveyed the truck, I kept my distance, hoping she wouldn't smell the beer on my breath. We couldn't see much. There was definitely damage, a piece of roof pushed up. But the truck was too high to get a good angle.

Traffic had thinned out. The sun was going down, but there was still light. Let's go up on the bridge, Cara said. Check out the damage.

By the time we got to the top of the steep hill to the railroad tracks, I was sweating. In the fading daylight, I could just see the streaks of red Georgia clay on the knees of my black work pants. I turned, helped Cara up the last bit of hill, and we walked across the gravel to the center of the bridge.

Shit, I said, looking down at the truck, surveying the damage.

I looked over at Cara, but couldn't read her. She's always had a remarkable poker-face.

Shit, I said again. *Shitshitshitshitshitshitshit...*

It's okay, she said. It's fine... accidents happen.

So what now?

Well, corporate policy is we have to get an accident report.

But there's no other cars.

Still...

Cara, I said. I don't have a license.

3.

Everybody has always told me I'm too smart for my own good. So smart I'm dumb is what they mean. My parents have been especially fond of this trope. For instance, I scored really high on my SAT, then repeated senior year because I skipped class so much. Which (being enrolled in work-study so that half the day I wasn't even supposed to be at school) was an achievement that greatly confounded my Dad. But it seemed Coach Fraser's history class had done me in.

Those who fail to learn history will be doomed to repeat it, Coach always said, and it never ceased to make me knot up with embarrassment for him. And after I remarked that all the world's problems could be solved with better history teachers, he wasn't inclined to round up my 69.4 average, even after I had rallied with a 99 on the final exam.

This from someone who got a near-perfect score on the SAT, my Dad had said, pacing the new hardwoods he'd had laid with his work bonus.

Hungover, I reminded him, sitting backwards on the heavy oak kitchen chair. It was too wide to sit in that way, but at that particular moment, it seemed an appropriate sacrifice for a necessary nonchalance.

I don't get it, he had said. You only had to show up for three classes.

Really two, I reminded him. The first one was for college credit.

My mother furrowed her brow, tightened her lips. Her eyes alternated between me and my father's shoes. I've always said it, she said. He's too smart for his own good. Then, to my father: Careful, Jim, don't scuff the new floors.

Or at 21, when I decided to move to Athens on a kamikaze mission to win my girlfriend back, and I ended up staying, just hanging around the bars after she refused to see me. I'd called home after a month to hopefully hit them up for a loan.

What's in Athens? my dad had said over the phone.

It's a college town, I had offered.

You're not in college! he said. You couldn't get in there with your grades, remember?

I laughed. I knew he was trying to piss me off. When high school was over, it had been like a mass exodus to UGA for my friends.

Beth's here, I said, meekly, the words catching in my throat.

I thought you broke up... What's in Athens, son? For you, I mean, he said finally, his voice equal parts tenderness and parental concern. It was as genuine as he could be. I hated him for it.

I got a lead on a job, I lied.

What are you going to tell your kids? my mom said, another one they were fond of repeating. She had picked up the phone in the other room. What are you going to say when they ask why you didn't go to school?

That I always felt I learned more from spring break?

I tell you Louise, my dad said. He's too smart for his own good.

Jesus, Dad, really –

I bet that's what Beth got tired of – one too many snappy comments.

This was in those quaint days of landlines and payphones. I distinctly remember turning away from the payphone to the late afternoon traffic on Broad Street, then turning back to flip off the mouthpiece of the phone.

Well, I said. I'll call you guys when I have a place to stay.

I hung up. I didn't get the loan I'd called for, but it was more important to not let them see I didn't know what I was doing. A good poker-face was important with my parents. If they saw I was worried, my mom would freak out. If my mom freaked out, my dad got mad. Then it just became melodramatic. So I learned to play it cool. Just walk away or hang up when they started saying their lines – when I felt it coming on.

Besides, I really hated hearing how smart I was. It had been all I had ever heard about since they stuck me in the gifted school in junior high – even after I flunked out for not keeping up with the work. But anyone could be smart. Or appear smart. It was all confidence, anyway. Picking up on the right things contextually, and re-wording it so it sounded like what people wanted to hear. Politics, essentially.

Bullshit, essentially.

4.

When I think about how long it took me to figure out why Cara got me that job at The Holiday Inn driving the catering truck, it doesn't make me feel particularly bright. She was pregnant. We'd only slept together once, after being friends for nine years, so the night she told me about the job, I just thought she was falling for me.

We had been drinking at Barcode until late. I sold cocaine to the bartenders there, and we were drinking for free after hours while the staff closed up. When the chairs were stacked, I would rip out the personal stash and cut one out for everyone on the neon bar tops. *Like doing lines in a lava lamp,* we'd say.

So what are you gonna do? Cara said. You're gonna need a real job for probation, right?

I guess, I told her. But I'm more concerned about losing my license.

Some weeks earlier, I'd been pulled over and arrested for DUI. I'd played it right I guess – or it was the end of the shift – for whatever reason, they didn't search my car. Still, I was in some shit. I got a DUI attorney from one of the billboards around town, pled guilty, and paid a fine to get it over with. I had the money. I got off with a year of probation and a suspended license. I owed Cara big for driving to my house in the middle of the night to get my stash of cash hidden in the attic and then coming and bailing me out – and on the night of her Biochem final too.

Ashton got a limited license, she said. To go to work and school.

I downed a shot of Jamie's, chased it with a High Life. I pulled out the personal stash, dipped the house key to my parent's place in it, held it up to Cara. She put her hand up.

Got to work tomorrow, she said.

I nodded.

I guess I have to get a job, I said, doing her bump. *Fuck* though... that blows.

C'mon, you've been saying you needed to stop selling for a while.

Cara had been my best friend since junior high. After flunking out of the gifted school, it had been like none of my friends remembered me when I came back to my home school. Cara had been new, and we sat together in Language Arts. We did a project on the Greek gods and hubris – one of the few A's I got post-elementary school. We'd always had a good thing going. We were friends because she was one of the few people who could care yet stay detached enough not to worry. This was an important quality for people who loved me.

But a month or two back, after a night of heavy drinking, I'd gotten Cara to do a line with me when we got back to her place. In the past, she had refused to touch the stuff. We sat Indian-style on the living room floor next to the speakers, playing the stereo extra low, so it wouldn't wake her roommates.

Finally, the light was coming through the living room window.

I can't believe I'm not tired, she said.

Good shit, huh?

You know what I want to do? I looked her in the eye, saw that look girls will get sometimes.

What? I said, after a minute, forced a grin.

I want to build a fort.

A fort? I laughed.

Yeah, in my room, y'know... like when you're a kid. With blankets and pillows... A place that's safe, where no one can get at you, or find you.

All right, I said. Let's do it.

So we got the rest of the beer from the fridge, got some extra blankets and pillows from the hall closet, and went in her room. We stacked pillows, hung the blankets from her closet door, tucking them in between her mattress and box spring. Under the fort, we shared the last three beers in silence, feeling the heat from each other.

G*d, I really want to make out right now, she said. I know it's a bad, bad idea. Like incest or something, but—

I kissed her.

Like kissing my brother or something... she murmured.

I kissed her again.   This time, running my hands through her hair, pulling her head back, kissing her neck.

I stopped, looked at her.

Shut up, Cara, she said.

It started off well, but quickly became awkward. Both during and after. I hadn't called her for a couple of days to let it wear off. Then, we went out for beers, agreed to never talk about it again, and that was that. But that night at Barcode, when she told me about the job where she worked, I realized something I had been picking up on the past few times we'd hung out. She kept catching herself, before saying something she knew she shouldn't. Like without meaning to be, she was invested. I thought she must be falling for me. She had a history of reading too much into sexual encounters with the guys she'd been involved with.

Look, she said, sipping her beer. You said you've been looking for an excuse to stop selling coke. Is there a better one than legal troubles?

But the money is really frickin' good.

How many felonies were in your car the other night when I bailed you out?

I nodded.

Look, it's up to you. We're hiring at the hotel for people to work catering shifts. They're looking for guys right now because none of the girls want to drive the truck.

What about my license?

I'm the assistant manager, and Tony loves me, she said. He'll hire you. You just work on getting the limited license.

I didn't say anything.

It's 12 bucks an hour... pretty good.

She didn't know I'd been making three grand a week. I remember when Ashton hooked me up with my first eightball of coke to sell, he laughed. I had looked at him, and he had told me be careful – selling coke was more habit-forming than doing it.

All right, I told her. I'm in.

I looked at her, grinned.

For you, I said.

Oh, fuck you.

I laughed.

No, thanks, Cara... really...

The only thing is, you can't fuck this up, she said. I need this job.

I got you, I said. Don't fuck it up.

We touched beers, I took a long pull. Again, she sipped.

Gotta go...

She stood.

Go? What'd you have? Two beers?

Just the one.

And you didn't finish that? Weak.

She shrugged. Cara was sketchy about coke, but she had always been a drinker. Still, I didn't think about it much.

Call me tomorrow, she said, halfway to the door. About the job, I mean. She paused. If you don't change your mind...

Good night, Cara-bear! Her dad had called her this growing up.

She flicked me off, went out.

5.

But I never did get the work-to-home license. When I got
the job, I hadn't surrendered my old one yet, so I let Tony
make a copy of that. It turned out, the restricted license took
a judge or something, and you only had a certain amount of
time to ask for it. I don't know why my lawyer hadn't done
it, he seemed busy. Anyway, I missed out. It seemed
complicated. Besides, I had never been pulled over since I
was sixteen. The DUI had been at a roadblock, and
roadblocks were late at night. I mostly worked in the day.

For the first month I was working, I quit fucking
around with powder. Not even recreationally. I cut my
drinking in half, and I was eating at least two meals a day. I
gained weight. I ran into Beth at the Kroger, and we talked,
decided to go out for dinner. She was really pleased I had a
good job. We started dating again, but it was too weird. Ever
since she had been pregnant the summer before, it was like
she was afraid of sex. Or maybe just sex with me – because
I heard she was seeing another guy for a while.

The night she broke it off for good, we stood in the
parking lot of her apartment complex after dinner. I had
been trying to get her to let me come in.

Imagine losing a part of yourself, she said, finally.
Imagine cutting off your own dick.

I know, Beth, I said. But it was your decision. I just supported you.

I know, she said, her voice breaking. And that just makes it worse.

I stood there, trying to think of what to say. It was hard, because she wasn't a crier. Not like some girls.

You never even said what you wanted to do, she said.

She wouldn't look at me. I realized there was nothing I could say. She had wanted me to tell her to keep the baby, and I hadn't.

Beth had been the one thing I did right. Even my parents had always agreed with that. They always hated Cara ever since they caught us the summer before senior year with a twelve pack and a quarter of weed. My mom had always wondered what kind of girl only has friends who are guys. But when I started dating Beth, they loved her. And I did too. She was smart, beautiful, kind. It's a wonder she's with you, my Dad joked more than once. But now, there was obviously no going back. On the way back to my place, I called Ashton.

What's up, man? he said.

Not much, I told him. Got to work early, but still... not tired.

Want to tip the bucket?

Sure.

Well, I'm up, he said. Come on by. The next day, I worked an engagement party after two and a half hours sleep. Cara had been off, and everyone else I worked with wasn't savvy enough to know the difference.

It's not like I went off the deep-end or anything. It wasn't my every day like when I had been selling it. It was still the plan to keep the job until I went off probation. And I knew when I met with my PO, I'd have to piss clean. It was simply that, without Beth, being totally straight felt like pretense. There just wasn't a point to it.

6.

When we worked that wedding that afternoon, I hadn't been high in a week and a half. Cara had been there, a whole crew of us had been. The bride had a meltdown during the reception – about what wasn't too clear – and the party kind of fizzled out. So we were off early. We had cleaned up and were loading everything in the truck when Ashton paged me.

I called him back.

Where were you last night?

Sleeping... I told him. Had to work, remember? A wedding.

It's my birthday, man!

It's not your birthday until Sunday.

It started last night, though... and who gets married on Easter?

Who throws a keg party?

Me, that's who. His birthday had coincided with Easter and Spring Break that year, so he was throwing a three day party in honor of himself and the Resurrection of the Lord.

How was it? I said.

It was sacrilicious. Tabby sewed this little doll to look like me and they nailed it to a cross, hung it over the kegs. Then they made me do keg stands 'til I couldn't anymore.

The Passion of Ashton...

He laughed.

Well, we got half a keg left until tonight. Dizzy's gonna get three from the restaurant for tomorrow, but that won't be until morning. Stop by, quick...

I got to finish up, I said.

Dude, you gotta help me... Save my life: Whit just spelled out *Happy Birthday Ashton* in coke. For the *third time.*

I was standing at the catering truck, using the truck cell phone. I looked at Cara. She and Katie were getting in Cara's car. I knew she was going to drop Katie off at her apartments on the other side of town. And they had talked about Cara going in for a minute to get a text book she needed next semester. Ashton's was between the reception and the hotel. I had at least an hour before needing to get back to unload.

All right, I told him. I'll stop in for a minute.

7.

Three hours later, I was up on the railroad bridge with Cara, staring down at the big, white catering truck. It's roof was peeled back like the lid of a sardine can. Shit, I said.

So what happened with the limited license? she said.

I... I tried, I told her. I really did. It was complicated.

She didn't look at me. She had been playing it cool, but that was all she could take. It had to happen at some point. She had this thing like Beth used to get when I disappointed her, like my mom and dad −like, if she didn't look at me, it wouldn't touch her.

*G*d, I fucked this one up*, I thought. *I can't believe I slept with her.* We went back down the hill, sliding part of the way on our asses. At the bottom, I tried to help her up, but she wouldn't take my hand.

Let's get out of here, she said. Then, forcing a smile: *I'll* drive.

She's trying to cover it up, I thought. *Trying not to care. Damn, this was a cool girl. Not melodramatic, not afraid to drive a truck. I can't believe I fucked this up – and after nine years.*

We rode back to work in silence. I stared out the window, watched the blur of scenery. I felt strangely sober.

We pulled into the empty parking lot, and she parked the truck in its space. I looked over, saw her face. I could tell the whole ride, she had just been getting madder and madder. She got out, caught herself before slamming the driver side door.

I sat there, not knowing what to do. I listened as she went around the truck, opened the back. I heard her climb up and in. I was feeling edgy again, from the powder at Ashton's, and I wanted a drink to balance me out. After a while, I went around to the back, saw her standing among the folded tables and chairs, towards the back where the bar was braced next to the boxes of liquor, wine, and beer. She was looking up at the rip in the roof.

What? I said.

She didn't answer. I climbed up into the truck. When I came near her, she laughed to herself.

What?

Nothing, she said. It's just – it's been a fucked up month. Grab a couple of chairs. I pulled a couple of chairs off the rack, set them up. She rifled through the boxes, the bottles rattling. She pulled out a bottle, set it on the bar. Then, she found two glasses.

We need a drink, she said, pouring two out, then handing me one of the glasses.

I sipped. It was scotch.

Damn, I said. Smooth.

18 year.

Well, we might as well go out in style – seeing as we're fucked.

We?

Me, I said. Seeing as I fucked everything up.

I'll tell them I was driving, she said. Katie was the only one left at the reception when you drove off, and she'll keep it quiet. She's got a crush on you, you know.

Cara...

What? I should let you go to jail?

Cara.

Tony can't let this go. He can't. Any damage to the vehicle, he has to report to the DM.

The district manager was Rob. Well into his thirties, he was what those of us in our twenties called a lifer. This was his career, and he had that malicious corporate loyalty that you find in those guys who got sucked into being something that they never wanted to be – like they became adults and the world didn't need any more policemen or firefighters, but there was a shortage of dickhead Holiday Inn district managers and he fit the mold.

Why would I go to jail?

This happened a year back – this guy Chris rear-ended someone in one of the trucks. The bumper was just slightly bent. The other guy was in a truck too, but there was no damage, so they didn't call the cops. When Rob found out, he made Tony call the police, and Chris got cited for leaving the scene.

Fuck, what a piece of shit.

What do you think is gonna happen when they find out you're on probation? That you've got a suspended license? I know I'm not Beth, and I'm not your mother, but I have known you – what? Nine years? I can't watch you go to jail.

Cara...

But she wasn't listening. She was looking at her glass like she was trying to decide something.

Month? I said, after a minute. Why a fucked up month?

I assumed she had been talking about us sleeping together, then this, but we had slept together longer ago than that. It could've just been a misstatement or maybe she was talking about work, but no.

It was how she said it.

We sat in silence, sipped whiskey we couldn't afford if we had to pay for it ourselves. At least I did. Cara was staring in the glass like she was watching someone tiny drowning in it, trying to decide whether or not to pull him out with her god-like stature, deciding whether or not it was really her job to intervene. I looked up above us, and through the roof, peeled back, were the stars, bright and dilated.

It was gorgeous.

I'd never seen anything like it. And I realized, since the beginning of time, no one, anywhere, had seen the stars from this perspective. There were people out there who had them all mapped out, people who could identify the entire sky. And here I was with this particular view, someone unable to locate any constellation, not a single one. It always seemed to me that you could connect the dots anyway you pleased, really, but seeing them now, from an angle only I could own, I wished I knew what I was looking at so I could say later: There was Orion, or there was Pleiades – right there above me through the roof of the truck peeled back like the lid of a sardine can.

Shit, I laughed, bitterly.

What?

I was thinking about my father and mother now, what they were going to say when I called from jail. I looked at Cara.

I'm just thinking what my parents would say...

What's that? Her tone was flat, benign.

My Dad, he would say: *Too smart for your own good, son.*

Smart? she said.

Yeah, I laughed.

There was a short, thick silence.

You're not as smart as you think you are, she said. You know that, right?

Yeah, well... it's easier than just admitting you raised a dumbass.

Then, I stopped replayed what she had said, heard it.

Wait, me? I don't think –

But I didn't finish because I realized I did think it.

Was proud of it even.

And my mom, I went on. Mom would say: *What are you going to tell your kids when they get old enough to ask?*

Yeah? she said. She was looking up at the stars now too, and I was wondering if she was seeing the same thing I saw. Then: *Why* didn't you wait on me to get there? I told you to *wait...*

You did?

On the phone... I said, I'm on my way, wait for me before you do anything.

I don't remember.

Jesus, all we had to do was let some air out of the tires!

I stopped. I looked up again, and we were quiet for what felt like a really long time. The night sky and all the unlearned constellations demanded it. Awe. Or reverence, maybe. Something.

I'm sorry, Cara, I said, hoping my voice wouldn't crack.

It did.

Even though she had to have heard, I was glad it was dark.

It's all right, she said, then added: It has to be, right?

I'm sorry...

So what? she said, finally. What are you going to tell your kids about this – when they're old enough to ask?

Nothing, I said, quietly. You don't tell your kids shit like this.

Sure you do, she said, looking up through the roof again. You have to let them know that you're human. That you fuck up. Because they're human, they're going to fuck up too.

I followed her eyes back to the sky. She reached over, took my hand. We hadn't ever touched each other much, other than that night, and the hand was cold, distant – not unlike the stars we were looking up at. The longer we looked, though, the closer, the warmer, they seemed.

So what? What do you tell them? I said. What's all the fucking up for, anyway?

Well, she said. If nothing else –

She laughed to herself.

What?

If nothing else – what a view of the stars!

A DIFFERENT DEFINITION OF DIRTY

This guy I work with – Rick Barr – asks me to get a beer after work. I run into him in the head around three o'clock, and he tells me something happened last night, that he's got to talk to someone. I'm washing my hands, talking to his brown leather wingtips and khakis under the door of the stall, so I don't ask for details. I tell him to find me at quitting time.

I don't socialize with people from the office much, but Rick insists on being the exception. When I first started, he helped me getting a handle on my accounts. Ever since then, he asks me to go to lunch a couple of times a week, and sometimes we'll get a drink after work. He and his wife Jackie even had my girlfriend and me over for dinner a few months back.

Rick likes talking to me because I'm young. He's in his late-thirties, which is not necessarily old he's quick to remind me, it's just that he's got a wife. I tell him I've had a serious girlfriend going on two years now. He says it's different though, and I'll understand when I'm married.

But do yourself a favor, he always tells me. Don't get married.

After work, we go to this bar around the corner, The Cotton Mill. I've brought Rick there a few times now. He's got a thing for Erin, one of the bartenders. It's a nice place with wood-paneling and good-looking waitresses that dress in all black. It's more of a restaurant really, but I like the bar there because it's a step up, and there's good food if you get hungry. Plus, they know my drink and what specials I like.

Tonight, it's Mike tending bar. I sit down, and he uncaps a Coors Light in a bottle, no glass, and puts it front of me. He asks Rick what he's having. Rick asks for a Bud Light, and Mike and I make some small talk about the ACC. We both root for Tech in spite of the futility.

When another customer comes in and sits at the other end of the bar, Mike goes to get him a drink. I ask Rick what's up.

I had an affair last night, he says.

What? I swallowed my beer a little too quick and choked.

It's not that I put it past him for a second, but I called him last night for some information about an account I was taking over. He had given me a hard time for bugging him about work, saying he was watching the Late Show in his shorts.

Well, I almost did, he says. I was this close. He holds up a small space between his index finger and thumb. I would have been caught, so I had to wait.

Jesus, Rick – with who?

This girl at the condos.

Rick and his wife have a two-bedroom condo on the ground floor of one of those new communities they're throwing up everywhere. You know, the ones that have restaurants and grocery stores and a movie theater.

What girl?

I don't know, this girl who I see sometimes. He stops, looks around. Looks just like that bartender who works here – the hottie –
what's her name?

Erin.

Yeah, Erin, he says a little too loudly, and looks around again.

Erin's got dark hair and blue eyes, full breasts, and perfectly-rounded hips. She's got this punk thing going on with tattoos and a little nose stud, only she makes it look classy. She can talk to anyone in this way that makes you feel like you're actually interesting, like there's no other customers in the room as far as she's concerned.

Personally, I like this other waitress named Maria a little better. She works in the dining room, but she brings food to the customers in the bar sometimes, and occasionally, I try to flirt. Rick says she's hot, but he thinks Erin would be better in bed.

He takes a pack of cigarettes from his jacket pocket, pulls one out and puts it in his mouth.

Let's go outside so I can smoke, he says.

We get another round from Mike and go out to the front. There's a patio for bar customers with two or three tables. It's not busy yet, so there's no one out there.

As I said, I'm not really shocked. Rick's been looking to cheat on his wife for a while. He's always talking about how he and Jackie are having problems. He tells me about it at lunch. One time a week or two ago, as I was about to cut out a little early for the day, he cornered me. We ended up talking in his cubicle until 6:30 about whether or not he was the kind of person who was *meant* to be married.

As we sit down, he starts by reminding me about his problems with Jackie. It's always the same sort of stuff. Jackie wants to get a house, Jackie wants a kid (even though she agrees they can't afford it). Jackie won't do the kinky stuff in bed anymore. She says she doesn't like it like she used to.

We want different things, he says. We're two different people.

My favorite is how Jackie gets upset because he won't ever clean the bathroom. He says she likes things cleaner than he does and gets to it first. Can I help it if I have a different definition of *dirty*? he asks.

I just shrug and think, *Asshole.*

The real problem is that Rick sees other good-looking women and doesn't know how to deal with the fact that they're off limits. He flirts with them, and they respond, and he starts imagining a different life for himself. But there's a certain amount of confidence a guy has when he has a girl to go home to. It makes him extra charming to women in elevators, waitresses, and strangers in bars.

The sad part is that Jackie is a great woman. She's tall and thin with long, curly auburn hair. And maybe Rick and I have different priorities, but she's got the nicest shaped hips and ass I've seen on a woman. Her breasts are small, but as you get on in years, you don't want a chick with big, saggy tits anyway. She's smart and easy to talk to. She watches sports, even follows them. Her father was a high school football coach, so she knows even more about football than Rick does.

But, then again, sometimes I don't think Rick likes sports. He pretends to because it's something guys are supposed to like.

Anyway, we're sitting outside drinking our beers, and I watch him light up. That's the latest thing she's upset about, he tells me, that he's started smoking again after promising he'd quit. Last night, Jackie found a cellophane top in his pants pocket doing the laundry. He really only quit for three weeks, but he didn't get caught for nearly six months.

So what about the girl? I ask. Where did the girl come in? It sounds like you were home with Jackie all night.

I was, he says. But we were fighting all through dinner, and afterwards, she went in the bedroom, so I stayed out in the living room.

Okay... and the girl?

It's this girl I've run into in the parking lot a couple times. After dinner, I took the trash out to the dumpster, and I saw her.

They have this thing, he says, he and this girl who looks like Erin the bartender. When he passes her, they look each other in the eye and smile, speak even. But last night, it had gone a little further.

Trash duty? she asked him.

'Fraid so, he said.

And she smiled all sexy: *Maybe you'll do mine, next.*

After that, he made some lame joke, and she laughed a little too hard. But I didn't think much of it, he says. Especially when I came back, and she was gone. He did, however, notice the porch light was on up on the second floor of the building she went into. He went back inside, and Jackie was in the bedroom, so he sat on the sofa watching sitcoms. After a little bit, I called, and when he got off the phone, he felt tired, so he got a cigarette and went out on their small, covered patio. From there, he could see the balcony where he had decided the girl lives. The porch light was off now, but he was looking up there anyway.

That's when he saw the flicker of a cigarette lighter.

He lit his cigarette, staring up at the dark balcony. The darkness, he says, was magnetic. He kept looking back, and it would pull him in. And after a minute, he says, he could feel her looking down at him. He stared so long he saw the embers from the tip of her cigarette.

You probably imagined it, I tell him.

No, he says. One of the parking lot lights has been out for the last week, so it was dark out there. Then he tells me that in darkness you can see the light from a cigarette for miles. He says that it's been a problem in warfare for years.

So there he was, staring at the embers of the cigarette he saw, or imagined, whatever, and he felt her watching him in the dark. Not only that, but after a minute, he says, he started to hear her whispering to him.

It sounds crazy, I know, but it was so real. I know I couldn't have heard it from where I was. It was more like it was telepathic or something.

Whispering? Whispering what?

I don't know. It wasn't so much like actual words. It was just flirty shit.

I look at him, narrow my eyes.

It's just like, *Hey there*, and stuff like that.

Hey there?

Yeah, and *Nice night out*. But not actually, it was more like her thoughts were prompting mine.

At this point, I'm shaking my head thinking: *You'd better be picking up the tab, Rick,* but I let him go on. I'm starting to get a little uncomfortable, but the last thing you want to do is tell a crazy person they're crazy.

I mean, I know it was in my head, most of it – I know that, he says. But something did happen out there.

Yeah, man. If you say it did, I'm listening.

No, really, buddy. I'll tell you how I know.

He says at that point, he had finished his cigarette, but he wasn't ready to go inside, so he lit another. Then, after a minute of standing there smoking in silence, no telepathic communication, he sees the lighter across the parking lot flare again.

Then he got an idea. He flicked his lighter on, and then let it go off. Nothing happened, so he did it again – three quick times.

Nothing.

He was about to put the cigarette out and go inside, when he saw the lighter on the balcony flicker once and pause. Then it flashed three quick times.

He smiled. He flicked his lighter twice.

A second later, the lighter on the balcony flicked twice. He waited a minute, then did it another three times. The lighter on the balcony did the same. He says they did this off and on for half an hour. The whole time, he says, there's this tension – this erotic tension – welling up inside of him.

There's a car horn from the street, and I look and see a long line of evening traffic in front of the restaurant. At least I'm not in that, I think.

Rick lights another cigarette, the third since we came out.

It was the strangest thing I ever experienced, he says.

After a little while, they stopped. Then, a minute or so later, he saw the lighter up on the balcony flick two times, extra short.

It was goodnight, I knew it!

He says he flicked his own lighter once, as if to say, *Wait,* but he knew it was it was too late. I didn't know what I was expecting, he tells me. It was so intense. It was like I was trapped in the present or something.

Trapped in the present?

Yeah, that's how it *felt*, like it was destiny. And then: her light came on.

The shades were drawn, he says, and there was no one out there, but there was the light on the balcony. An invitation. He looks at me deadpan, exhales smoke from the corner of his mouth. He said he sat there thinking of something he could tell Jackie, knowing that he had to go soon or not at all.

I mean, things like this don't happen to guys like me, he says.

I want to tell him that they do if they don't take medication for it, but I turn my Coors up instead, finish it off.

Rick proceeds to tell me how he concocted a story in his head about needing to take a walk. He says he knew Jackie would take that to mean a cigarette, but that she would be so irritated that she wouldn't suspect anything else. So he went back inside, put on his coat, and straightened his hair in the mirror by the door. Then he started to open the front door, but thought better.

He went into the kitchen and opened the cabinet where they keep the liquor and took a big swig out of a bottle of rum, nearly puked from the aftertaste. Then he went back out to the patio and climbed over the railing. Because the parking lot light was out, he didn't have to worry about Jackie seeing through the window.

What were you thinking would happen? I ask him. Sex? I mean you can smell it on someone afterwards, at least women can – especially if you're lying in bed with them.

I figured I'd come straight back in and shower. She would wake up, but it would support the cigarette thing even more.

I shake my head.

Look, I wasn't thinking clearly. Obviously. But things like that don't happen to guys like me. What would you have done?

I shake my head again and laugh.

C'mon, what?

I honestly don't know, I tell him. I probably would have thought I was going crazy and not had the balls to go over there.

And that's what it sounds like – that I was going crazy. But I tell you brother, I knew. I just knew.

Yeah, I say. So what happened? You go up there, and her husband answered?

No, he says. I told you I was sure. Anyway, she doesn't wear a ring.

But you do. Just because she was flirting doesn't mean she wants you to cheat on your wife with her.

I'm telling you, man...

Still, it's one thing to flirt with a married man. It's a whole different type of girl who sleeps with one.

You're not getting it, he says. It's not *about* types of girls. There was a connection there.

Okay, so why didn't you do it? You said you *almost* cheated.

Yeah, well the thing is, I did cheat... He looks down at the bricks that make up the floor of the patio like he's ashamed. In my heart, I did.

Okay.

It's the same thing, he says. I went up the stairs and stood in front of the door. I wanted to knock, but I couldn't. I just stood there.

He finishes his beer, puts it down on the patio table. He lights yet another cigarette, continues: After a minute, the door shifted, and I jumped. I could feel an eye on me at that point, through the peephole. I felt like I was on fire. I had to knock.

So you knocked?

No, he says. But I might as well have.

What? Why?

Because I wanted to...

That's not the same thing as doing it.

It is when the only reason that I didn't was I was scared that Jackie would know. I basically cheated.

Man, that's not cheating. You punked out.

Of course I did, he says. But it's not about punking out. It's about what I wanted. I wanted to cheat.

So what, you feel guilty?

I feel like a fucking heel, man.

Why? You were scared she'd find out because you don't want to hurt her. You did the right thing, I tell him, though I couldn't help thinking I would have respected him more if he had the stones to knock, crazy or no.

I guess, he says. I hope.

I think so, man, I say, hoping to end the conversation.

After all, what more can you say to a guy like that, the sort of guy who believes everything is destiny, who believes that he's *trapped in the present*? Whatever that means...

The thing is, he says, I feel like I already did it. And if she's out there again, tonight, I should just go through with it.

You actually think she will be out there again? Flicking that lighter?

I don't know, but I have a feeling...

He's finally done smoking, and I say we should go back inside. I order another beer from Mike, but he says he has to get home to Jackie, and he wants to stop off and get her flowers. I stifle a laugh because he says he's buying the beers.

When he's gone, I order dinner. My girlfriend already told me she had plans, so I figured I might as well. After I eat, Maria, the waitress that I think is cute, comes over. She's off work, so she sits at the bar counting her money to separate her tips. She's got thick, curly black hair, dark olive skin, and a perfect body. We flirt back and forth, and she says that she's going for a drink at this bar around the corner.

I tell her I can't, that my girlfriend is coming over.

Too bad, she frowns.

I pay for my dinner and go home. At home, I take a shower while my girlfriend's on the way. Thinking about Maria, what could have happened if I had called my girlfriend, told her I was going out with friends, thinking about what might have happened with Maria had I met her at the bar, I jerk off.

Later, lying in bed, my girlfriend starts rubbing my crotch, but I'm not in the mood. I keep picturing Rick, waiting out on the patio, flicking his cigarette lighter in the dark, hoping Jackie won't come out and see him. I wish there was something I could have told him. But a guy like that is going to do what he's going to do. Some guys just need problems so bad they create their own.

HOMEOWNERS INSURANCE

Standing on their front lawn in the middle of the night, their house on fire, he was in pajama pants, t-shirt, and slippers; she was in sweatpants and a tank top, her arms crossed in front of her. She shivered, even with the heat from the flames. He went over to the Audi where he had moved it to the street after it started, opened the trunk, and found an old pink quilt he kept to lie down on, in case he had to change a tire. Also in the trunk was a French horn she hadn't played in six years and a photo album her grandmother made for her as a girl.

He came back, wrapped the quilt around her.

When the fire trucks arrived, the upstairs was already engulfed in flames. Flakes of ash caught the wind, floated onto the lawn. The first fireman down from the truck looked at him, started to say something, but instead went to work.

He imagined the inside, itemized each room. The Horchow sectional sofa she had to have, the Waverly fabric window treatments. For him, it was the Canali suits, the Ferragamo loafers, the Breitling watch. Stuff. He hadn't risked saving anything for himself, not even the direct-to-disc LPs his father had given him, and he hoped when she saw the horn and the photo album she would understand.

Slowly, neighbors appeared on their porches and manicured Bermuda lawns. He imagined looks of concern cross their face as they thought how it could've been them. *It had been an electrical thing that started in the attic,* he imagined the investigators saying. *It had caught the insulation, some cans of polyurethane, and there was nothing anyone could do... it's the shoddy way they build houses these days.* Two neighbor boys were outside on the porch with their parents. They jumped up and down excitedly in their pajamas. Their father yelled for them to go inside.

He turned back to his burning house, thought how he never liked this neighborhood. There were hardly any trees.

They sat on the front porch of their across-the-street neighbors, a retired couple. He had never spoken to either of them. He'd waved a few times to the husband when taking out the trash, but that was as far as it went. Now, the husband was inside making them more coffee, the wife comforting his own wife. He felt the heat of the fire, even all the way across the street.

Come inside, the neighbor's wife said to her. You don't need to see it.

But I do, his wife answered. Strangely, I do.

Still wrapped in the old quilt, his wife sat on a whicker porch chair, holding her mug with both hands. He remembered, once, dating, they picnicked on that quilt on the lawn of the office park where he had worked. She'd brought him lunch. People passed from his office, gave him strange looks. They had taken off their socks and shoes. He remembered saying something funny, and she had laughed so hard she snorted and was embarrassed. Then, he had kissed her, her lips still strange to him, still new.

The neighbor's wife patted her on the shoulder, went inside. His wife got up from the porch chair, came over, and stood next to him.

He was thinking about a lot of things at once. He thought the glow from the flames on her face reminded him of the glow on the face of someone watching television in a dark room. Only more natural. Then, he thought about their cat that had run away a few weeks ago. How, earlier, he was so sure the cat wasn't coming back. Now, he found himself afraid the cat would. He thought about her credit card statements he'd printed, left on her dresser, the charges from the in-town hotels circled in red marker. He'd been so proud to finally find proof. He never thought she'd just leave them there, not say anything. *What?* she said, when he finally asked. *It's not exactly like you've been the eternal flame of fidelity.*

He thought about her back before law school, so unassuming, so captivated by his charisma. Somewhere along the way, he felt they had switched places, and that was the problem: he had always had an easier time being strong for someone other than himself.

He thought about the unpaid bills piled on the kitchen counter, how if all went well, they'd finally be paid. How if not, it wouldn't matter.

Kindling, he thought.

And the mess. When they first moved in, they'd cleaned together every weekend, proud of their first house. He'd vacuum, she'd dust. She'd clean the bathrooms, he'd do the laundry. Lately, though, the laundry collected into piles on the laundry room floor, and the tub had a dark ring neither one of them had the strength to scrub out. They fought constantly now over getting a cleaning lady. He always swore he'd never pay for someone to clean his house or wash his car even if he could afford it.

Maybe this could be a chance, she said, though she was looking at the burning house. To start over... I mean maybe this could be a way to...

Like fore-*closure*? He turned to her, smiled. She laughed shortly, the first time they shared a joke in months. She looked at him. He knew she knew. He pulled her to him, held her.

I guess now we don't have to worry about cleaning this weekend, she said, her face buried in his chest.

Across the street, firemen were running around. There were three trucks and hoses, but no one seemed to be doing much. He felt the hysteria rise in both of them simultaneously. They were laughing. He pulled back, put his hand under her chin, and lifted her face to look at him. He kissed her softly, deliberately, on her lips – the lips of a stranger. The wind picked up, the flames made one last grasp for some unseen thing above.

Then, the roof fell in.

THE DNR

Coming down the street, right before it crossed over to the dead end where we lived, I saw the animal lying on the side of the street. It was ginger-colored, and I knew right away it wasn't a raccoon, or a possum, or anything that was supposed to be dead on the side of the road. I didn't even think about the possibility that it was my girlfriend's dog until I crossed over the busy street at the light, pulled down to the house we rented, and into the driveway.

I got out of the car and walked all the way back to the fence that jutted out from the house and ran around the backyard. The gate was open. It was fall and becoming cooler out, so I went in and checked anyway, hoping maybe she'd left her inside.

Honey! Honey-bear! I called. Honey! Come get a cookie!

I opened the jar of dog treats we kept on top of the refrigerator – the sound of the ceramic scraping against itself invariably brought her running. Sometimes I'd get home on colder days when we left her inside and try to open the jar quietly enough to keep her from hearing. It had never happened.

I stood there holding the treat in my hand, not wanting to think about what came next. I looked at the clock. It was 3:15. I had an hour before my girlfriend got home from the elementary school where she taught. I got in my car and drove back up the street and pulled off to the side of the road. I crossed the street and almost got hit by an Oldsmobile that had been behind me the whole way. It honked.

Fuck you! I yelled after it. Fuck you!

Standing over the dog, I was afraid to touch it. It looked cold and distant, more like a grass-covered stone lying in the gutter than a dog. I bent down and put my hand on her. The fur felt fake to touch, what with the lack of warmth or movement.

It was her face, though, that made me cringe. Her mouth, slightly open, had a small trickle of blood running down the corner. Her eyes were open, staring off into nothing, into the vacant lot outside of the abandoned warehouse across the street. We lived across from the old Industrial District, where they were turning all the old factories into lofts, in a neighborhood of houses that used to belong to the factory workers.

I reached over and tried to close the dog's eyes like they do in the movies.

Fuckers! I screamed. Couldn't have stopped? Could you?

There was an old man sitting on the porch two doors down. I looked at him for a moment, and he didn't move. He just sat there rocking. Finally, I went to the trunk of my car and pulled out an old blanket that we would sit on when we went to the park. Honey and I had napped on it a hundred times in the shade while Carol roller-bladed.

I brought the blanket over and spread it out on the ground. I picked her up in my arms and sat her on the blanket as gently as I could. Once I had her wrapped in the blanket, I put her in the back seat. I drove back down the street to the house.

I knew what I had to do. Carol had made it clear a dozen times. I thought of the night we met. We'd had such a good time at the bar that she invited me back for a nightcap. As I followed her down the street, I knew what was going to happen. Neither one of us were given to one-nightstands. We'd found the ones we'd had to be drunken and awkward. So on the way back to her house, I had been trying to think of a way to politely leave after the drink, and she had been thinking of a way to ask me to go. We admitted that to each other sitting on the couch, and I had realized two things. I had almost finished the beer she had given me, and I didn't want to go.

That's when Honey came to the rescue. She wandered into the living room to see who the stranger was in her house.

I found out later she had been locked in with Carol's roommate because she had a tendency to be over-affectionate with strangers. She had gotten out when the roommate had left the door cracked going to the bathroom.

You have a dog, I said.

Oh yes, Carol smiled. This is my Honey-bear.

Honey was a golden retriever, but she also had that sandy, reddish color like an Irish setter. She was licking Carol's face.

She's my life partner, Carol said, taking her black-rimmed glasses off to clean them. Don't judge.

She sat there and smiled awkwardly at her own joke. Her hair was still blonde then. Since we had been together, she let it go back to her natural dark brown.

I laughed and asked how long she had Honey. That's when she explained that Honey had been her father's dog first. He had died a little over six months before.

Honey is all I have left of him. I don't know what I'd do if anything ever happened to her.

The way she said it – the vulnerability, yet her voice was completely steady – it seemed like more than she would admit to just a stranger. We spent that night together, and two months later, when her roommate moved out, I moved in. Countless times since then, whenever we saw a squirrel or a skunk on the side of the road, she would cringe. Once, we saw an old shag carpet lying with the trash at someone's curb, and she covered her eyes thinking it was a dog. She couldn't take it if something like that ever happened to Honey, she would say.

Then, looking in my eyes: *I just couldn't bear to see it.*

I checked the clock on the dash pulling in the driveway. I only had a little over half an hour. I opened the back, picked Honey up, and brought her out in the backyard behind the old, rusty shed. I got a shovel out and walked around and started digging in the yard between the shed and the fence. I dug as fast as I could. If nothing else, for the last two years, I felt like I owed Carol this. Though I had never made it verbally, this was a promise I could keep. She wouldn't have to see her father's dog stiff and lifeless. I knew we would have to get a good marker for it, and if we ever decided to get married, we would have to buy this ratty old house, but I didn't care. This was one thing I could do.

I patted the last of the dirt down just as the sun went behind the trees. I went inside and found my phone on the kitchen table where I had left it looking for Honey earlier. I had 2 missed calls from Carol.

Hey, what's up? I said, calling her back.

I was calling to tell you I was running late, she said. But that was an hour ago. We had conference night, so I had to stay a little bit later.

I looked at the clock. It was just after five.

Where have you been?

I was outside, I said. My phone was on the table.

She didn't say anything.

I was outside, Carol, on the porch. Are you on your way?

Yeah... I'll be there in about 20 minutes.

Okay, I'm going to shower. I think we should go out for dinner tonight.

All right.

Okay?

Okay...

I love you. I'll see you when you get here.

I hung up and stripped off my clothes. I had been coming home from my Wednesday lunch shift at the restaurant where I worked and had never changed. I balled them up, took them to the laundry room, and put them in the washer. I was still going at the harried pace I had been since I got home. I wanted to be dressed and ready before Carol got there.

I knew what she was thinking. She had recently found out that I had been seeing this girl, Rachel, the bartender at my work, for the last two or three months. After a lot of tears and screaming, I had promised to break it off. Carol and I had decided to work through it. The problem was that whatever it was wasn't getting worked through, and two weekends ago, when Carol was visiting her mother in North Carolina, I slept with Rachel again.

The night I met Carol at the bar two and a half years ago, I had the day off from work. I spent it walking around this old historical cemetery in the city, sketching and writing in my journal. Afterwards, I had gone out for a beer. She was sitting next to me at the bar, and I had struck up a conversation with her after she asked to see my sketch book. I remember she was drinking a beer straight from the bottle, something I'd always found sexy. Telling her about my day had gotten us on the topic of death and being buried. I told her that I wanted to be cremated because I had an irrational fear of being buried alive. She said that as long as I had a plan for my ashes, it was okay.

I looked at her funny. That was when she first told me about her father.

My father was cremated, she said. His ashes have just sat on my mother's mantel for the last six months. She doesn't know what to do with him.

Your father died six months ago? Jesus, I didn't know...

It's all right, she said. The only thing I'm afraid of is that one day no one will know what to do with him. He's just been sitting on the mantel. And what if she never does anything, and when she dies, what if I don't know what to do? And what if my kids don't? What if he's passed down from generation to generation until nobody even remembers who he was?

I didn't know what to say to that, so I asked how he died. She told me he had a bad heart – that it had quit and he had spent the last few months on life support.

That's awful, I said. That's another thing I'm afraid of, being tied to a machine.

You should be a D.N.R.

What?

She took her wallet out of her purse. From the wallet she brought out a laminated piece of paper about the size of a driver's license and handed it to me. It read, *ATTN: HEALTHCARE PROVIDERS I have created the following advance directives.* And below there was a form she had filled out with words like Living Will and Power of Attorney.

What's this?

It's my D.N.R. card. Do not revive, do not resuscitate.

I didn't even know they had these things.

Sure.

Resuscitate?

Like C.P.R.

Yeah, I know. But what if you're swimming and you hit your head and start drowning?

You don't revive me. I don't want to risk brain damage. To me, unless I'm whole, I'm not alive.

So your father's death made you do this?

No, I did it a couple of years ago, she said. It's just something I've always wanted to be.

Yeah, I laughed. Some kids want to be teachers, some astronauts. You wanted to be a D.N.R.

She laughed.

Not exactly, but kind of...

In the shower, I kept replaying that night in my head. It occurred to me as I cut off the water that maybe she was taking the same philosophy now with our relationship.

She was home when I got out of the shower. I heard her in the kitchen and walked out wrapped in a towel to greet her. She was standing in the kitchen, a glass of red wine in her hand.

Hey, I said.

Your work clothes were done. I put them in the dryer.

Thanks.

You know, I did laundry this weekend. You still had three pairs of pants and shirts for this week.

Yeah, I know.

So...

So?

Why do a load of laundry for one pair of pants and a shirt?

Carol, it's not what you think.

It's not? It sure looks like it.

Carol...

You didn't even bother to change your M.O.

What?

You never knew that's how I figured it out, did you? You'd come home at three in the morning after – and I quote

– drinking with the guys, and take a shower and wash your clothes.

Carol, I –

A man who did one load of laundry in two years all of sudden is doing his work clothes every night.

Carol, this isn't right.

You're damn right it's not.

 No, I said.

Look, she said. I'm going to take Honey this weekend and go to mother's place... I need you to pack up and go stay with your folks while I'm gone. Tonight and tomorrow you can stay in the guest room.

Carol.

No, no someone should have pulled the plug on this thing a while ago. She paused. I just wish it would have been you, you know? Before?

Then she stopped talking and looked around.

Where's Honey? she said.

I tried to tell you, I said. The gate –

What happened?

I –

What happened to Honey? she whispered.

Friday night, when I got home at midnight, she was gone. The note said she was at her mother's through Monday. It was fall break at her school. That was all it said. But the imaginary post script told me I could either go up after her or pack up my things and go to my parents. I had to work Saturday night, so I didn't go up then. The restaurant was closed on Sunday, so I planned to go up in the morning, but I never did.

Sunday night, I was sitting on the porch on top of the last of my boxes, putting off loading them into my car. After a little while, I worked up the courage to call her and say goodbye. I went back inside and picked up the phone that hung on the wall in the kitchen.

It was strange hearing the dial tone. I never used our landline, I always used my cell, and the constancy of it reminded me of those TV shows where the doctors lose somebody on the operating table. On the EKG – which I didn't even know what that meant, just what it was called – there was the flat line, and the accompanying tone like a dial tone that meant the patient was dead. I started to dial, but I couldn't remember the number. I could have gone out to my car and looked it up on the cell phone, but I didn't.

I leaned back against the wall and listened.

UFOs

1.

Some time before we'd get the call that Ben saw his face in the sky, that he believed that he had a police escort on his way out of town to school, he sat on Jared Prince's mom's roof, improvising quiet solos on the electric guitar. We had to unplug at midnight. Prince's mother was asleep down the hall, so the patch cord lay lifeless just inside. This was somewhere in the suburbs, somewhere in America. This was the summer after high school, maybe a year before we would visit Ben at Ridgeview.

He was famous then, or soon to be. And we were all coming along for the ride: Prince playing keys (once he learned them), Lenny on back-up vocals and percussion. Then, of course, a roadie was needed, maybe someone to write lyrics. Not to mention bass and drums, but those were problems to be solved in the future.

Those nights, Ben would be strumming the guitar. Lenny, the only one of us who had gotten into college, would be there too, usually passed out on the bed: the world's premiere punk rock valedictorian. And Prince, of course, always at the ham radio, the one that belonged to his father before his father got some waitress pregnant and disappeared when Prince was in ninth grade. There were some others: Neal Anderson who drank two bottles of cough syrup on his seventeenth birthday and woke up in his parents basement, sleeping in the crib he used as a baby; or Jimmy Island, whose older brother sold weed and Lucy, their parent's house rumored to be under surveillance by the FBI. Many rotated in and out through various days of the week, various hours of the night, but it was always *us,* and we were always a little bit lost, a little bit insane – and Ben, always the nucleus.

We honestly thought it was Prince who would start hearing voices – reference his addiction to conspiracy theories (The Smoking Gun bookmarked at the top of his favorites) – that, even though he wouldn't admit it, he was actually searching for extraterrestrial life on that radio, or – perhaps more astronomically still – for his father. He would sit in his room for hours, turning the knob by degrees, while Ben would feel out a muffled riff on the roof just outside.

That summer had something to do with searching, surely, but frequency too: both of which are functions of time. We didn't have jobs, we were out of school, there was never anything to do, yet always there was this pervasive feeling of waiting. And always, in the distance, the moon an unidentified flying object, and beneath it, a red light flashing from a cell tower in the distance. We didn't talk about it, but it was sending us a message: something about sleeping through every day. Something about nights spent dreaming.

2.

We sat on the roof of Prince's mom's house, just outside his bedroom window, passing a joint, the red light on the cell phone tower in the distance, flashing messages.

We ignored it.

There are things you just don't talk about, Prince said, much later – he was referring to Ben – but it holds true for a lot.

Prince had taken a break from the radio to join us on the roof. Lenny was already passed out on the bed inside, snoring. Someone, probably Prince, made a joke about him having been the valedictorian.

Ben was trying to teach Prince to open a zippo and light it in one fluid motion.

Practice, Ben told him.

He put the electric guitar – a knock-off Fender Strat – to the side, showed Prince one more time. His face was briefly illuminated, long, handsome, gray-eyed, goatee like a smudge of dirt on his chin. Then, it went dark. He handed Prince back the lighter.

Ben taught himself to play with only a book of chords, on an acoustic guitar he found in his parents attic. A year later, he was writing songs. By next spring, though, we'd come out on the roof, and he'd only be playing a single note over and over again.

For a long minute in the dark, everything went silent, even Lenny's breathing. Then, Ben laughed, a sharp, mirthless laugh.

Hah!

What? Prince said, failing at the lighter. What's so funny?

Ben said nothing, and we let it go. That summer, Ben still knew something we didn't.

There's another way to look at it now, the inappropriate laughter, the long silences: *signs*. Either way, he was tuned into a frequency we couldn't receive.

I asked what's so fucking funny, Prince said.

He sat straight up.

Ben laughed again.

Prince tossed the lighter at him.

Just because you don't get the joke, Ben said, doesn't mean it's on you.

Man, what the fuck are you talking about?

That's when we heard a loud siren behind us, threading its way in the dark through the hills of white houses, through the safe, American suburbs, locked up tight for the evening. A deafening sound came down around us, closing in: rising, whirring. An increasing wind. At first, we thought it was terrorists, or maybe the Chinese.

Then: a blinding light shining down from above.

Prince dived through the window. Moments later, he stuck his head out with Lenny, awake now, beside him looking out.   Ben just sat there like Buddha, barely looking up, almost like he had been expecting it to happen. ~~And me, I still can't tell you whether it's sadder to have been taken in by the mother-ship or to have been left behind on the ground.~~

No one quite agrees on what happened that night. Whatever it was, it was not what was reported in the official story. We would go on to college, get decent jobs, married, mortgages, kids. None of us talk to each other very often anymore. Lenny calls Prince every year on the day Kurt Cobain died, but we're light years from where we were. That summer, without actually talking about it, we were trying to decide what was the worst that could happen when and if something ever finally happened.

When and if we ever discovered life out there.

THE NAMING OF CATS

But above and beyond there's still one name left over, / And that is the name that you never will guess; / The name that no human research can discover–/ But THE CAT HIMSELF KNOWS, and will never confess.

–T.S. Eliot, The Naming of Cats

1.

Park Bench was a restaurant on Briarwood, in a trendy neighborhood where the late twenties/early thirties professionals went to spend their salaries once they were finally beginning to get out from under their student loans. One of the oldest restaurants in town, Park Bench wasn't quite as trendy as the rest of the neighborhood. It had a strange mix for a crowd. All day long through the week, they would get the business crowd and the neighborhood people with their kids coming in. But after eleven, the restaurant part shut down, and the bar that was open until after two had a whole different crowd come in. It was a lot of late-night types, waiters, and staff from other places around that closed early. There were the regular deadbeats and dart throwers, and usually someone at the bar trying to make back his tab selling dub bags of coke.

Michelle worked behind the bar at Park Bench and as soon as I met her, I knew I wanted a job there. She was tan with shoulder-length blonde hair, short and voluptuous, usually dressed in something black and low-cut to accentuate her breasts and to slim her waist and hips, which were soft from a propensity towards beer and an aversion to exercise. She once told me that she had never ran for any reason, and she always seemed relaxed enough that I believed her. She wore horn-rim glasses like all the hipsters had been wearing the last few years, but she needed them to see, and she wasn't so easily classified. She was a few years older than me in her early thirties and had a deep, coarse voice, nearly hoarse from smoking reds since she was fifteen. That was the most attractive thing about her to me – her voice – it was sexy in its casual weariness and made you feel like you were playing opposite some legendary leading lady in a black and white film.

I walked in off the street at three in the afternoon one day, and saw her behind the bar. The place was deserted. I looked around at the wood paneling and finishes. It was old and scratched up, but at one time it had been very nice, and it still retained a certain oaken elegance. There was discolored white-and-black-checked tile on the floor that would have provided a very classy look a decade or two ago.

Hey there, she called from across the bar. She wiped down a wet streak with the rag she kept hanging from her back pocket. Get you something to drink?

You could, but I need a job worse.

A job?

Yeah, I've been looking all over. I thought I had picked the wrong part of town before I saw this place.

What do you mean by that?

Nothing really. Just seems like a place I wouldn't mind hanging out is all.

She frowned.

I didn't mean anything by it...

Relax, she laughed. I know what you mean. But I don't know if we have anything open right now.

Really? I reached in my pocket and pulled out a folded up piece of paper. I stopped by yesterday, and they gave me this application. They told me to come back in today and talk to – I unfolded the piece of paper where I had the guy's name – Steve.

She laughed again.

What?

That's your application? All folded up?

Honestly, I've never seen a restaurant manager look at one of these things at any place I wanted to work at. I don't do the corporate places.

That's cool, she smiled. I didn't even know we had job applications. We don't take a lot of walk-ins.

Oh.

Well, she said. I got good news and bad news for you.

What's that?

Steve's off today, and I'm not sure he really needs anyone. What position did you want?

I was looking for bar work. I'd be fine to start as a server though.

Yeah, see, I don't know if there's anything available.

Hell, I'll take anything you got.

How'd you decide to come in here? Just walking around?

Kind of... I sort of know a girl who works here, or worked here. At least she did as of a couple of months ago.

Who?

Her name is Carrie.

Oh, you know Carrie? She's my roommate.

Like I said, I sort of know her.

She told you to come in?

Well, not really. I dated her best friend from high school. We lived together until a few months ago.

She said my ex-girlfriend's name.

Yeah.

You were with that girl?

Yeah, I laughed.

Sorry, I don't mean anything by it. I only met her once, it's just—

I know what you mean.

Man, small world.

I guess. Look, I said finally. If there's no jobs and Steve's not even here, what's the good news?

I'm buying you a beer for your troubles. What do you want?

I ordered this ale they had on draft, a choice that seemed to impress her. She stood across the bar, talking to me about beers she liked as I drank it. She was easy to talk to, and when I finished the beer, I asked her for another she had been telling me about. She wouldn't let me pay for that one either, because of the runaround.

Well, I said. I guess I'll see you around.

Wait.

She took a pen from behind her ear. She made some quick scratches on a cocktail napkin, handed it to me. There's a party at Steve's house tonight. Carrie and I will be there. Come by, we'll introduce you.

That's really great, but I don't really know Carrie that well – we only met a few times. I can't ask her put herself out there for me like that.

You know me, though. And I'm offering.

Okay, then.

I reached out and shook her hand. Then I felt stupid for doing it and half-stumbled out of the place.

After I left Park Bench, I drove back over to my friend Rick's apartment, where I had been staying since my girlfriend and I had decided to end our lease and our association simultaneously in the same month. I was sleepy from the beer and the afternoon sun. I went straight for the couch and went to sleep.

After a little while, Rick came home and asked me how the job search was going. He was sick of having a roommate. I had been giving him some money each month that I borrowed from my Dad, but it was a one-bedroom place, and after two and a half months, it was getting cramped.

Fine, I said. Just fine.

I closed my eyes and managed to fall back asleep.

2.

I got to the party around 10:30. It was in a neighborhood near the restaurant, and the house had a bunch of cars out front. There was a group of people sitting on the front porch, but no one I knew.

A guy with too much hair gel and one of those shirts with the horses on the breast pocket greeted me.

How's it goin' bro?

All right, bro, I said. You live here?

Not me.

I'm looking for Michelle.

Blonde chick? Works at the bar?

Yeah.

She was in the kitchen.

The people on the porch were mostly drinking beer from plastic cups, though a few of the women had glasses of wine. I figured there was probably a keg of beer around somewhere.

It was in the kitchen. There was a big crowd of people, most of them a few years older than me, likely college graduates and professionals. There was a group of guys, jeans and button down shirts, crowding the keg. I saw a pair of legs in the air and two more guys, each with as much hair gel as the first I'd seen, counting off.

I rolled my eyes involuntarily and felt a little embarrassed for them. Looking up, I caught Michelle looking at me. She smiled and shook her head. I made my way around to her. She was sitting on a counter littered with empty cups and open wine bottles, drinking a beer.

She hopped down when she saw me coming in. She looked gorgeous, wearing blue jeans and a white blouse open at the neck. It was one of the few times I would not see her dressed in black.

Waiting in line for a keg stand?

Who, me? No, she said. And for a second, I thought she was embarrassed because she thought I was serious. I already took one, she grinned.

Oh yeah?

Three actually.

Three keg stands, wow.

Well four if you count the one where that asshole dropped my legs.

Fucking drunks.

I can't believe they're doing this. It's such a frat boy thing to do.

They must be reminiscing.

Must be, she said. It's not like it's Bud Light or something either. It's a pretty heavy beer.

What is it?

She told me, but it was some German or Belgian name that I couldn't quite get the pronunciation of. She gave me a sip of hers. It was a good beer.

The guy came down from his keg stand and stood looking confused for a second. Then he stumbled over to the sink right next to me and threw up.

I guess you don't want a beer now, she laughed.

She took the last drink of her beer and picked up a half bottle of red wine, open on the counter. I tasted it. It was a good wine, especially to drink straight from the bottle.

Let's go elsewhere, she said. This is degenerating fast.

Okay.

Bring the wine.

The kitchen was on the back of the house. We walked back through the dining room and into the living room, navigating little clusters of people. The place was nicely decorated with matching furniture, curtains, and everything. The sofa and chairs were still thick with padding so that if you sat down, you were sitting a little bit higher than you were used to. There was even art on the walls.

Let's find Carrie, she said over her shoulder. I told her you were coming, and she got all excited.

She surveyed the living room and then took my hand and led me outside. I didn't know what to think about Carrie being excited to see me. She didn't see my ex-girlfriend very often, so we never knew each other very well. One time we had all drank too much wine at our place, and Carrie had told me that if I ever wanted to get a job at Park Bench, I should come see her. I had figured she wouldn't even remember.

We found her on the porch. Carrie walked up and gave me a big hug and a kiss on the cheek.

Hey, sweetie! How are you? She said it too loud, and the whole porch of people turned around.

I'm all right.

Uncomfortable, I wanted to say. I don't even kiss people I'd call my friends.

There was something else about her that made me uncomfortable all the way around, something I had forgotten. She was a kind person, and not all together unattractive, but she had an overbearing quality that really grated on me. She was short, with reddish-brown hair that fell just below her chin. She had green eyes, a nose that was a little big for her face, and slightly crooked teeth, but a nice complexion. She was tan and very fit, her arms and legs were chiseled from jogging and lifting weights. She once described herself to me as a JAP (Jewish-American Princess) from the suburbs turned big, city girl. That was about all I knew about her, but she was one of those people that are always a little bit too familiar with acquaintances.

Where's your drink?

Um, we're sharing. I was referring to the bottle of wine I had handed back to Michelle.

Where are your glasses?

Oh, we don't need any of that, I joked. I was afraid people were still looking.

You're drinking it from the bottle! Omigod!

Shocking, I know.

I just can't do that. I love wine too much, she said. I have to sip it.

That was another thing I remembered about her. She knew very little about wine, but liked to act like a connoisseur.

So how's life? she asked.

It's life, things fall apart – you put them back together.

Yeah, I heard you moved out.

I lost my job too.

At the Italian place?

Yeah.

Oh, no. What happened?

It closed down. Funny thing about not paying your taxes. I'm going to use it as an excuse to get back in school.

You're in school?

No. I need a job and a place to live first. I've been crashing on my friend's couch.

So you came into Park Bench?

Pretty much. I'm supposed to meet this guy Steve tonight.

Did Michelle not tell you?

Tell me?

I looked at Michelle.

I've got good news and bad news, she smiled.

Oh?

Yeah. Steve ran out to take one of the waitresses home.

Okay.

Well, he probably won't be back tonight.

Oh.

Yeah. He kind of does that sort of thing. All the waitresses love him, and he breaks their hearts.

Sounds like a helluva guy.

With a guy like Steve, it's a little bit on you if you don't see it coming.

I'll look out for that, I said.

Carrie laughed, accidentally snorting.

He took Cherise – the new girl – home, and they seemed *pretty* chummy.

I guess that's good news for Steve. What's the good news for me?

You start at ten tomorrow morning.

You're kidding.

Nope, we talked to him before you got here. He said you sounded like a good guy.

Well, I appreciate the lie, I said.

The only thing is, it's kitchen work. Expediting, back-up on dishes.

Setting up plates and shit?

Yeah and making salads, Carrie said. You only make minimum wage, but you get tipped out. And he said as soon as there's a server position open, he'll try you out.

Sounds good, I said, trying not to sound reluctant. I didn't know how I was going to afford my own place on minimum wage, and I had no ideas for roommates, but any job at this point was better than none; *and* there was the question of proximity to Michelle.

But I don't get to meet 'ol Steve and thank him for the opportunity?

Not tonight, Michelle said.

So he has roommates, or he just ran off and left all these people at his house?

Carrie rolled her eyes, and Michelle looked away.

What?

See that woman over there? Carrie asked.

She was pointing at a blonde woman in her mid-to-late thirties, very attractive, sipping a glass of white wine and talking to a big group of people.

That's his roommate?

That's his wife: Rachel.

After a while, we left the wine bottle and went inside and got beers off the keg. I drank a couple, talking with Michelle and Carrie.

I wanted to try and be alone with Michelle, but Carrie could not take a hint. She was drunk and kept rubbing up against me and laughing too loud at everything I said. I was buzzed though, and she seemed nice enough in spite of her being a little bit grating. There would be plenty of time to get to know Michelle.

I left around one in the morning, after meeting some people I would be working with – mostly waiters and bartenders. There was only one other guy from the kitchen staff, a Mexican guy, who worked sauté and spoke perfect English, but I impressed everyone by speaking Spanish with him. Even he seemed impressed at how much I knew. But it had been so long my pronunciation was awful.

I would have stayed later, but I didn't want to get drunk and stay up too late, then have to learn a new job in the morning, so I went home. Rick was sitting up on the recliner, next to the couch where I slept, waiting for me when I walked in. There was no music, and the TV was turned down. He was just sitting there. I could tell by his look that we were about to have that talk.

I got a job, I said.

Oh, really? He was skeptical.

Yeah, I start tomorrow morning at ten. I was just out meeting some people I'm going to be working with.

No way.

Yeah, tomorrow at ten.

Cool, man. Where at?

He seemed genuinely interested now. Less like he was my father.

Park Bench. It's on Briarwood.

Oh yeah. I've seen that place.

Yeah. I'm excited.

I'm going to get a beer from the fridge, and you can tell me about it. You want one?

A beer? Sure.

But I thought about it and realized something. This was the first time he had talked to me like a real person, like a friend, in weeks. To hell with him, I thought.

Actually, on second thought, I need to get to sleep.

Oh, yeah? I guess so.

I went over to the couch. My blanket was folded over the back of the sofa. I unfolded it, and covered up. Lying back, I rolled over and closed my eyes with him still standing in the doorway between the kitchen and the living room.

One thing I learned not having my own place is that you can learn to sleep under any conditions.

3.

For the first couple weeks, I didn't work with Carrie at all. Steve, whom I finally met (he turned out to be the asshole I expected), scheduled me during the day, and Carrie worked at night.

I didn't like Steve very much because he had the impression that because I didn't want to talk about sports or pussy with him I was retarded. It was okay though, because he was the type of bastard who would be very vindictive if he didn't like you.

I didn't even mind that he wasn't going to move me from the kitchen to waiting tables anytime soon either. The expediting was growing on me. I learned more about what goes into making the food. There was a kind of art to it, a rhythm I got into, and at any rate I didn't have to shave every day, and I wore comfortable clothes, black kitchen pants and a black Park Bench t-shirt . I've had plenty of wait jobs and even jobs tending bar, and I can honestly say that the best part of kitchen work was that I did not have to talk to anyone I did not want to, excluding Steve. And with him, my money didn't depend on how well the conversation came off, as long as I pretended to make an effort liking him.

I was busting my ass and doing a good job too. It was the first work I'd done in a few months, and it felt good to be in a new place and on my way to having some honest money again. I did such a good job that when the Brazillian guy who worked nighttime quit, I replaced him.

I think I've found my calling, I told Michelle and Carrie sitting at the bar after my third nightshift. I had been working doubles everyday while they found a new daytime guy.

Oh really, Michelle laughed.

Don't say that, Carrie said. You're so smart, and you need to go back to school.

No, really. It's great not having to deal directly with customers.

Michelle went off to get someone a beer. The bar was still crowded even though the kitchen was closed.

You do, though, Carrie said. You need to get back in school. You're too smart to be a dishwasher.

She liked to refer to me as a dishwasher, as if it was something ignoble. It was part of my job to collect the dirty pots and sauté pans for the dishwasher and to help him when he was backed up. But Carrie had taken it upon herself as soon as she found out I was planning to go back to school to see that I did it. She is one of those people that think that a college degree is the answer to all life's problems. It's not that I wasn't sure her philosophy degree came in great handy waiting tables, but it wasn't really necessary to spend thousands of dollars when she could have gone to the public library and checked out a book.

And she was always telling me how smart I was as if college was the only place in the world for smart people. I had a good job, a new crush, and my tip outs at the end of the night usually afforded me enough for a few beers at the end of the night and the spending money I needed.

What I need first is a place to live, I told her. My buddy is getting awfully tired of sharing his sofa, even if I am paying half the rent.

He doesn't like living with you?

It's just cramped. It's a one bedroom.

Oh, that's right, you told me.

She smiled and looked into my eyes all bright and proud because she had remembered, like she somehow knew me better than anyone.

Well, it turns out I need a roommate, she said.

What about Michelle?

Well, she wants to move out. She's been looking to buy a place.

I didn't know that.

Yeah, it's been getting hard too. I don't like living with girls.

Michelle's not a girl. She walked by as I said that and looked over.

Damn right I'm not!

Omigod! I hope she didn't hear me! Carrie put her hand to her mouth.

Why?

I love Michelle, it's just – I just don't think I can live with her anymore.

You told her that?

No, but I think she kind of knows. That's why she's been looking to buy. And she's found a place she really likes.

So you need someone to cover the rent until the lease is up?

I regretted it as soon as I said it.

Well, not especially, but it would be nice. I'm trying to save up to buy a place too.

How long does the lease have left?

I was pretty reluctant. I did not want to live with Carrie. But since I had moved out of my parent's house at eighteen, I had always prided myself on being able to live with anyone who was not my father.

Six months. We renewed it in September.

How much?

400 dollars a month for you. I pay more for the master bedroom. The house is pretty small, though, so bills are cheap.

It would be tough to afford that on what I made, but it would only be a few months, and I needed to get off the couch.

When can I move in?

Well, I can talk to Michelle, maybe pretty soon. We have a third bedroom we use as an office, but there's a couch in there you could sleep on, if you need to go ahead and move.

You know, that would be great.

I don't know where you'd put your things though.

Honestly, I don't have much right now. What little I do have is in storage and can stay there a little bit longer. Hell, they probably won't even let me get it out until I have enough to pay them the money I owe.

Well, let me talk to Michelle about it. I'm sure she won't mind though. It will be really cheap until she moves out.

Thanks, Carrie.

I gave her a hug, and she kissed me on the cheek. It made me nervous, but I was feeling pretty elated. Not only would I be living with Michelle for a little while, but I had an out from my friend's couch. There is something about being an unwanted guest when you have no other place to go that just drains the soul. I could almost see how a person would rather sleep on the street.

4.

When the tension between my new roommates finally came to a head, it was over the cats. I had just lied down after being out with a friend, drinking beer and celebrating my first paycheck at the new restaurant job. He'd given me a bump of cocaine from his dub bag in the men's room, and I was having trouble getting sleepy. It had been nearly six months since I had a paycheck, and I felt good.

I was working a double the next day, so when I first heard the screeching in the hallway, I ignored it. The noises got successively more horrible and finally, I got up off the pullout bed to see what was happening.

Stanley, the fat cat, was easily overpowering Ming. Ming was an outdoor cat and a hunter, but Stanley had him on sheer mass alone. The only thing that Ming had going for him was that my roommate Carrie kept him de-clawed. Ming was scratching at him, but the larger cat had him pinned. Not knowing what to do, and possibly having a bias towards Ming because he was Michelle's cat, I kicked Stanley. This got him off Ming, and once separated, they ran off in different directions, Ming towards the front of the house, and Stanley to the back. He ran under Carrie's feet and into her room.

She and Michelle were now both standing in their doorways. Carrie was wearing a pink bathrobe and slippers, Michelle was in boxers and a Georgia Bulldogs t-shirt.

What's going on? Carrie asked.

Your fat fuck of a cat was attacking Ming again! Michelle shouted.

I stood, braced myself for what had been coming since long before I had moved in two weeks before.

Don't talk about Stanley that way! And how do you know Stanley attacked Ming? Stanley wouldn't hurt a fly!

Oh, fucking come on! He sits by the door all day long terrorizing him!

He does not! He sits there waiting for me to come home!

Oh, you are an idiot! He sits there because he wants to go outside!

I turned to go back in the bedroom.

Tell her! Michelle shouted. She was talking to me.

I stopped, turned slowly, and looked at Carrie, who had her hands on her hips, waiting for me to respond.

Well?

Carrie, don't take this the wrong way, but—

Oh, so you don't like Stanley either! You both hate my cat!

Oh, come off of it! Michelle yelled. No one hates your goddamn cat! He just needs to be let outside! You're killing his spirit, Carrie.

Just because I care about him enough to not let him run off, or get hit by a car, or to knock up floosies like your slut-cat does, doesn't mean I'm killing his spirit!

Michelle and I looked at each other.

Floosies? she said.

We broke down laughing and could not stop.

But we did hate Stanley. What was there to like? He was obnoxious as well as being grotesquely fat and a bully. When he wasn't sitting by the front door chasing Ming off, he would follow you around making noises trying to get you to feed him or pet him.

At first, I found him amusing. He was charcoal-colored on his back and sides and head, but with a white chest that made it look like he was wearing a suit jacket. He had big whiskers that somehow reminded me of a mustache, and I thought he looked like a fat, old maitre d' or a waiter at some fancy restaurant. Then I saw his temperament and the way he was to the other cat. I slowly became more and more disgusted by the nature of his existence.

He was an inside cat, and like most of the inside cats I had been around, he was spoiled and deranged. Inside cats always seem to have tendencies towards violence, whether towards people, other animals, or even themselves. Stanley was no different. Already I had come home from work a few times to find him banging his head on the wall near the front door.

His psychosis was only compounded by the fact that Ming got to go outdoors. Ming was the exact opposite of Stanley, compactly built and muscular, he was exotically marked in gray and tan with the most even temperament I have ever encountered in a cat. He was clean, despite spending most of his time outside. He rarely even used the litter-box Michelle had for him in the kitchen, unlike Stanley, who had no choice but to go in the litter box that Carrie was grossly negligent about keeping clean. When he did come inside, he would sit next to you on the sofa and wait for you to pet him, as opposed to the way Stanley would coo and moan and rub his head against you.

Ming was a hunter too, leaving rodents and birds eviscerated on the door step as little gifts to the household in attempt to contribute in his own way. This was Carrie's contention with him.

Carrie was an animal lover and in that strange, blind logic (or lack of logic) shared by a great many animal lovers, she could not recognize it as a sign of gratitude, despite Michelle and I trying to explain it to her. Instead, she thought Ming was some kind of cat serial killer, which was the reason she said she kept Stanley inside.

The other reason, which she didn't like to talk about, was that Stanley had belonged to her father, who died of a heart attack two years before. Michelle and I had talked about how that affected her logic, but it did not keep it from being any less absurd.

When the laughter finally subsided, I looked over at Carrie and she was sitting in her doorway with her head between her knees. At first I thought she was giggling, and I started to laugh again. Then I realized she was crying.

I can't, I just can't, she said in between sobs. What if something happens and he doesn't come back?

5.

The morning after, it was like nothing had ever happened. I woke up early for work and brewed some coffee while I walked across the street and grabbed the neighbor's newspaper. I was sitting at the dining room table reading it and eating a bowl of cereal when Carrie got up. She went in the kitchen and made a big breakfast with bacon, eggs, and biscuits without saying a word to me.

I was sure she would never talk to me again, but when her food was ready, she called to me from the kitchen.

You want some breakfast?

I just ate some cereal.

I made biscuits.

I'll have a biscuit.

She fixed me a couple of buttered biscuits with jam and brought them to the table with her plate. Then she went back in the kitchen, got some orange juice and some cloth napkins, one of which she sat in front of me. She sat down and asked to borrow the arts section. When Michelle got up, they were friendly with each other.

Are you working? Carrie asked Michelle.

Yeah, opening. You?

No, I have that interview today.

Oh yeah, that's right! Good luck!

Carrie had an interview with a small law firm for a paralegal position. Apparently she had minored in law, and had met one of the two partners in the firm one night at Park Bench. She was very excited about it. She had been a waitress for ten years now and was ready for a real job, as she called it.

Michelle was also working a double, so I rode to work with her. I would likely get cut earlier, but I didn't mind sitting at the bar waiting on her. I could mostly drink for free there, chat with people at the bar.

I had worked a double shift every day except Mondays the past two weeks, and I was exhausted. Fortunately, the job was still kind of new and exciting, and I liked the people who I worked with, so it felt good to work hard and be tired at the end of the day. The waiters and bartenders were all cool with me now and the guys in the kitchen loved me because I tried to speak Spanish with them, though usually with hilarious results.

Things with Michelle were going all right too. They were moving slower than I was used to, but that was okay. We would just hang out and talk. There was a mutual attraction I could tell, but neither of us had mentioned it yet. It was a little awkward living together, so I thought I would wait until she moved unless things progressed naturally.

They almost did one night. It was a week later, with still a week or two before she moved out. It was a Sunday, and we both had the day off. We had been working like crazy all week, so we were hanging around the house. I had paid off the storage place and got my room set up, and most of the office furniture was crowding the living room and dining room. It would go into Michelle's room when she moved out, but until then, quarters were cramped, so we decided to sit on the front porch.

We had a bunch of good beers in the refrigerator, and we were drinking them slowly because it was Sunday, and the stores would not start selling again until midnight. It was dusk and a pretty night, and if we were quiet, we could hear the faint sounds of the city from our neighborhood. It was early spring, the air was cool, and it felt good to be drinking beer outside.

Carrie came out and sat at the plastic table and folding chairs. She looked dressed to go out.

Hot date? I asked.

No, I'm going out with my friend. I have to blow off some steam... I'm so nervous.

About the job? Michelle asked.

Yes.

They still haven't called you?

No, and now I know they're not going to until tomorrow.

Why?

It's Sunday afternoon.

Maybe they'll call, I said.

They won't. I think I'll call them tomorrow, if they don't call by noon.

How long has it been since you talked to them last?

Three days. I'm going to call them tomorrow.

You should, Michelle said.

I mean, I have to know what to tell Steve about work.

A car pulled up on the street and tapped the horn lightly.

I'll see you later! Bye!

She ran down the porch and front walk and got into a beige sedan. The car pulled off blasting loud club music, all bass and cheeseball synthesizers. Michelle and I looked at each other and laughed.

I'm kind of buzzed, she said. The city was quiet, and her voice reminded me of car tires on a secluded gravel drive. Listening to her made the blood in my head hum.

Me too, I said finally.

You hungry?

A little bit. I should definitely eat something though.

Let's raid the fridge.

In the refrigerator, we found some chicken that was still good for a few days, so we cooked it up, put it over pasta noodles, and topped it with a sauce we put together from a half jar of marinara, Green G*ddess salad dressing, and some fresh spinach. We also had a bottle of red wine Michelle had won in a contest at work by selling the most bottles. We decided to eat on the porch and while Michelle was setting up the table, I set up the speakers in the living room, near the front window, so we could play music while we ate. When everything was ready, Michelle went back in because we had forgotten forks. While she was inside, she left the door cracked, and as I took a sip of wine, I heard it creak. I looked over, and there was Stanley.

He made a break for it. I leapt to my feet, lunged, grabbed him pretty roughly by the fat on the back of his neck. I pulled him back as he struggled and hissed.

Come on! I shouted. You know you're not supposed to do that.

Michelle came out with the flatware.

Did I let him out? she asked.

He slipped through the crack in the door, I told her.

Oh shit. Sorry.

Yeah, I smiled as I tossed the fat cat back inside. I bet.

Hey, if I was going to let him run away I would have let him do it a *looo*ng time ago.

I guess so, I laughed.

We ate dinner and talked shit about Stanley, avoiding the unpleasant parts of the conversation we knew we could fall into if we were not careful. We were both feeling the wine, and I let her talk as much as she would, enjoying the low engine on a long stretch of highway hum that was her voice, let it take me wherever it would. The meal was good for something so off-the-cuff, probably more so because of the really nice wine, and it left me feeling happy.

Michelle had been playing a bunch of soft, ambient-type music. We got along well when it came to music, though she knew a lot more about obscure bands than I did. We both loved Tom Waits though, and when the instrumental album she put on was over, I made her play *Heart of Saturday Night.*

By the time it was over, it was getting dark. I kept singing *(Looking For) The Heart of Saturday Night* even after it was over, a little bit drunk by then. I picked up the wine bottle and split the end between us.

Better take it easy, Tom, she said. It's Sunday, remember.

I laughed, looking in her eyes. She didn't look away, so I put my hand on her knee and ran it up her leg gently.

Are you flirting with me?

She smiled coyly and raised her eyebrows.

Maybe, I said, leaning in closer.

I had heard the car pull up a few moments before, but I had ignored it. It was now or never. I was going to kiss her when Carrie came running up the porch.

Omigod! Omigod! she shouted. I got it! I got the job!

They called you? Michelle asked, backing away.

On Sunday? I said.

Yes! she said. She fell in my lap and leaned over and hugged Michelle and then put her arms around my neck.

That's great, baby! Michelle said.

Congratulations!

Thank you, guys, she said and kissed me on the cheek. I was expecting her to get up and go inside at any moment, but she didn't. She sat there in my lap. I can't believe it! I'm so excited.

That's great, Michelle said.

Isn't it? Then she looked at us and the dishes and the empty wine bottle and the candle on the table. Am I interrupting something?

No one answered right away, but I think we all realized that she was.

We were talking, I said.

Oh, good! I want to be around friends tonight and celebrate!

Michelle went inside to get everyone a beer and to take some of the dirty dishes. She came back out before I could find a way to explain to Carrie that I wanted to be alone with Michelle. I did manage to get her out of my lap.

The three of us each drank that beer, and I had one more, before Michelle, who had looked pretty bored since Carrie had come home, stood up and yawned.

I need to sleep, kids, she said. I open up tomorrow.

G'night! Carrie said.

I'll help you carry the rest of the dishes in, I told Michelle.

We brought them in and put them in the sink. We stood there trying to think of something to say.

Just leave the dishes, I'll get them in the morning, she said.

No way, I told her.

You have to do dishes every day, I'll do them.

I know. I'm a professional. It's no problem.

You're sweet.

Nah...

Listen, I had a good time sitting on the porch with you.

Yeah. Me too.

Good night.

Michelle?

Yeah?

Good night.

She smiled and went to her room. I didn't want to talk to Carrie anymore, so I didn't go back outside. I washed the dishes and drank one of the last two beers. I had a clenched up feeling in my stomach from a lack of any kind of resolution, but at the same time I knew I should feel good that it seemed like things had gone forward, if only an inch.

Carrie came in and said goodnight and kissed me on the cheek. She was drunk and happy. I had finished the dishes and was sitting at the dining room table drinking my beer.

Stanley peered around the corner and stared at me. I called him over and scratched him behind his ears. Then I scratched around under his chest, and he grabbed on to my hand with his useless front paws and bit me.

Ow! Fucker!

I kicked him one time good, and he ran off to the other end of the room, over to the start of the hall. He hissed and ran off down the darkened hallway into Carrie's room.

6.

Things were going far too smoothly to last, and I knew it. I could see it coming. It's always happened that way for me. Every time things start to come together, something happens, and it all gets broken apart again. For a long time, I thought I was cursed. Since, I have tried to realize that it's just that life does not tolerate comfort, and that is why things fall apart. It is always the comfortable that die first – if not in body, then in spirit, and so I have tried to see it as a blessing, though more likely than a blessing or a curse, it is just life.

But when things fell apart with Michelle and the job at Park Bench, I truly felt fated for disaster. It was a Friday, a week or so before Michelle moved out. Steve had hired a new daytime expediter. Michelle had talked to Steve for me and convinced him to give me a shot serving. I was going to train that morning, and I would come back at five to pull the evening shift expediting.

The training went well. The shift was busy, and I ended up saving everyone's ass by being an extra. I ran lots of food and did not think, which for me, was the only trick to waiting tables, to act and respond without over-thinking.

Steve was there, and where he normally would have had to help the servers, he could stay in the kitchen helping the new expediter and the line. When he cut me, he told me I did a good job and gave me a pat on the back that wasn't even too condescending. It also meant I would probably get to take some tables in the coming weeks and make more money.

He left to go have lunch with his wife, so I sat at the bar and drank a couple of beers and talked to Michelle while the restaurant was slow. It didn't take much focus to expedite anymore, and I figured I could drink coffee before I went back on. Besides, there's not much better than the first drink after you finish a shift waiting tables. Even more than on a busy night in the kitchen, having to deal with people one-on-one – people in a hurry to get back to work, or to go pick up the kids from school, or people just plain hungry – it's one of the most nerve-racking experiences there is, especially knowing that the money you take home depends on so many circumstances outside your control, like the speed and quality of the kitchen, or even the customer's mood. It took a beer or two when all was said and done to set you straight again.

It went well? Michelle asked, standing across the bar.

I think so.

Steve said it did. When do you go back on?

Not 'til five.

Still, don't drink too fast. Steve would kill me if he saw me letting the new guy drink between shifts.

It was common practice for trusted staff to have one or two beers between shifts on a double, and it galled me a little bit to still be considered the new guy.

Don't worry, this is my last. Do you work all night?

I'm supposed to be early cut.

Yeah?

Yeah. I was thinking maybe we'd have a drink. Out somewhere, not here.

I think we should.

All right, then. She smiled and winked at me.

The dinner shift went fast while I still felt the effect of the beers. I had a big cup of coffee at the beginning of my shift which woke me up.

But by the end of the dinner rush, I was fading. I asked a waitress to make me an espresso. Then I cleaned up my area, and went around through the dining room to the bar.

Shift drink? Michelle asked as I sat down.

You know it.

What do you want?

I asked for a whiskey.

Pulling out the stops, eh?

It's been a long day.

Tell me about it.

Still want to go out?

She looked at me kind of funny.

What?

Give me a second, she said.

She went down the bar and mixed a drink for a guy who just sat down. While she did, I stepped over to the other end where Crash was sitting. Crash sold dub bags of halfway decent blow. It wasn't that Peruvian shit, but it wouldn't give you the trots. I slapped him on the shoulder, put a couple of tens in front of him.

Let me get you a round, I said, nodded.

I went back to my spot at the bar. A few minutes later, he came over on his way to the men's, thanked me for the drink, and slipped the powder in my shirt pocket.

Michelle got a highball glass, poured my whiskey, and came back over.

I've got to close now, she said, sitting it in front of me.

What?

Yeah, she leaned in closer and lowered her voice. Steve was supposed to close, but he's having marital troubles.

Go fuck-ing figure...

I know. I'm sorry.

What about when you get off?

I don't know.

C'mon...

She smiled.

You know you want to.

Okay, we'll have one drink.

Two.

Two, tops.

Sweet.

Don't drink too fast, she said.

I'll be fine.

I finished my drink and watched as Steve came out from the kitchen and over to Michelle.

I owe you big, I heard him say.

He walked by me on the way out, giving me another managerial pat on the shoulder. I rolled my eyes when he was gone.

I went to the men's room, did a bump in each nostril with my house key. Then, I went out for a walk around Briarwood while I was waiting for Michelle. I had a beer in a bar with live music and listened for a while, occasionally ducking out to the men's room.

I had a drink at a couple more places to kill time and made friends with some bartenders by making conversation and tipping big. I needed to save my money, but I figured bartenders were always good investments, as one drink can often equal two if you tip right. I was getting a second wind, so I spent the rest of the time walking around aimlessly, watching the good-looking women and their drunk, preppy boyfriends stumble in and out of cabs.

It was 2 a.m. when I went back to Park Bench. Michelle had just done last call. There was hardly anyone left, and I figured we could just make it over to this bar across town that stayed open until four.

Michelle offered me a drink, but I told her I would give her a little bit to catch up. She held up a half-empty beer glass, smiled, and made me one anyway, and herself one too.

Cheers.

I drank half of mine. She took hers down and chased it with beer.

I went to the bathroom, locked the door behind me and cut out a rail on the counter.

It was not long before the stragglers left.

The last two kitchen members walked out the back door, waving at us, while the late-cocktail waitress cleaned the last tables. Michelle had counted the drawer, and we were almost out when the phone rang.

Will you go around to the back and get my purse and jacket? she said, picking up the phone.

Sure.

I went around through the darkened kitchen and fumbled for the light switch in the back room. I found her things on the shelf and found my own jacket from earlier. It had gotten warm enough through the day that I hadn't needed it anymore. When I came back around, she was still on the phone.

Jesus Christ, Steve. Don't do this. I've got plans tonight.

I stood there and wondered if I should be listening.

She looked up and saw me, so I figured it was all right. She held up an index finger to give the sign that it would only be a minute.

Steve, c'mon, I'm tired, I don't want to deal with this.

What's up? I asked quietly.

One second, she whispered, covering the mouth of the phone. No, Steve, goddammit. You're being melodramatic. What, no, no. Look, I'll meet you for fifteen minutes, but that's it.

I sighed and shook my head.

Fifteen minutes, that's all. She hung up the phone.

I looked at her.

I've got to meet him, she said. He's crazy, right now. I'm worried.

It's not like he didn't bring it upon himself.

I know, it's just —

What? What is it?

Look, I'll tell you later. If you're still up when I get home, we'll have that drink.

Whatever.

Don't be upset.

I'm fine.

You're the best, she said, kissed me on the cheek. Maybe I'll see you later.

7.

You know they slept together, right? Carrie asked.

I had come home and she was drinking a glass of wine and watching TV. She was ready for bed in her pajamas on the recliner in the living room, when I had come in complaining about being ditched.

What?

They were sleeping together for the first year Michelle worked at Park Bench.

You're kidding me.

No, a year ago, she told him she couldn't do it anymore.

I can't believe it.

Why not? All the girls sleep with Steve.

All of them.

Not all of them, but the ones he hires do.

Did you?

No. We made out once...

Are you kidding?

Yes! she laughed. I'd never make out with Steve! That's gross! He's like my brother.

I just thought Michelle had more...

What?

More something, I don't know.

Steve's cute.

He's a chooch.

A what?

A chooch. He'a an asshole, and he's full of shit.

I know, he is. I hate it that he's like my brother.

I was standing in front of the couch, pacing back and forth. I stopped, looked at her, and shook my head. She smiled. I could tell she had been drinking before she had come home also.

You like her, don't you?

Hah, I said.

You can tell me.

If I did like her, I wouldn't now.

You do, don't you?

No, I lied. I'm worried though. Maybe I should wait up and talk to her.

Darling, she's not coming home.

You mean you think she'll sleep with him?

Don't be naïve, dear. What do *you* think will happen?

I don't know.

Are you sure you don't like her?

There's an attraction there, sure, I said. It's only natural though, living and working with someone you respect.

Oh? she said, and I realized then what I had said. Is there an attraction with me also?

I wasn't sure what to say. It wouldn't be accurate to say I found her repulsive. She was sweet and she had a nice body, but I knew the question was loaded with so much more than that. On the way home, I had stopped and bought a pint of whiskey. It was sitting on the coffee table. I drank the glass I was holding and poured another one. A few minutes before, I had gone to the bathroom and cut out the last small lines from my dub sack. I knew I would be up for a while, but I did it anyway. I never liked having any blow left over, it kept me from doing it two days in a row.

Sure, I said to Carrie, finally, without looking at her. It's natural, right?

Of course, sweetie, she said, standing up. You don't mind that I'm a couple of years older than you?

What do you mean?

She pulled me to her and kissed me. I pulled her closer and felt the curve of her breasts as they pressed to my chest. I ran my hand up from her waist and began cupping one through her shirt. She pushed me away.

This is a bad idea, she said.

Probably, I agreed.

She was toying with me. I knew she liked me, and this was her way of getting the upper hand. Either I start chanting romantic bullshit, or I pretend like I don't care – that's the trick – but even I'm not slimy enough to fake getting all romantic about something like this. That was some shit Steve would pull. I sat down on the sofa and waited for her.

We have to live together after this, she said, sitting down next to me.

I know.

But I don't see what's so wrong with it?

No?

If we fuck just this once?

I pulled her to me, and we kissed more. We fell back on the couch. She started grinding her hips against me.

Let's go in your room, I said. I felt weird saying it, but I wanted to be able to leave. I sat up and took another drink.

Let's do it here. She rubbed her hand over my crotch.

No, I said.

She won't be home tonight.

No, I told her and stood up.

She looked at me and waited. I took another drink. I took her by the hand and brought her down the hall to her room. I closed the door behind us and fell on her as I pushed her back on the bed.

Oh G*d, she said. Fuck me, baby, fuck me! She kept talking like that as we got naked and all throughout the process she talked dirty, and it was very loud. Part of me wished that Michelle would come home and hear us, and the other part of me just wished she would shut up. Finally, it was finished, and I rolled off of her and lay back on the bed. She curled up next to me and a few minutes later, she was snoring softly as the sick, gray light of dawn poked through the cracks in the window shade. I lay awake for another hour, spinning, waiting for the sounds of the front door and Michelle coming home.

8.

The sound of the front door creaking finally woke me up. It was just after 10 am. I could just barely see the alarm clock over Carrie's head. The house was quiet and every floor board in the place spoke as Michelle walked through the house. I heard the door to her room close and then nothing. My head was pounding. I did not even want to look at Carrie, which was hard because she was sleeping on my arm. I wanted to leave the house until I could get everything that happened sorted out.

The door to Michelle's room opened again, and I heard her walk into the kitchen. Carrie stirred and snuggled in closer to me. My arm started to fall asleep, and all of a sudden, I had to get out. It occurred to me that I couldn't leave if I did not want Michelle to see me, and that's probably what set it off. There is nothing worse when you are trapped than the realization of it. I imagined myself ready to start chewing through my arm quietly as Carrie slept on it.

Unfortunately, I would still have to somehow make it to the front door and out. I couldn't even sneak into my room because I had left my door open the night before. I had thought about closing it on the way to Carrie's room, but I told myself there was no point. I thought about the window.

But the windows in that old house were always stuck and would have made too much noise.

Just then, I heard Michelle walking again. The front door opened. I lay there waiting for it to open again, sure she was just going to her car or something, but she didn't come back. Quickly, I slid my arm out from underneath Carrie. She made a noise, and I lay back down for a minute. The last thing I wanted to do was face her. When I was sure she was asleep, I got up and climbed over her – my side of the bed was pushed up against the wall – and went quietly out of her room.

In the hall, I closed her door softly behind me. I walked quickly to the kitchen and made a glass of ice water. I drank it and filled it again from the tap, then drank it halfway down again. I walked outside and stood on the porch contemplating going out for coffee and something to eat, but it felt hot outside and my stomach was wrecked, so I went back in.

I went in my bedroom and tried my best to go back to sleep. The best thing would be to be unconscious for a while. It did not work. I felt a great anxiety like I had done something far worse than I knew, and it would not let me sleep. I pulled down all the shades and pulled the blankets over my head, but it was too hot, so finally I just lay there feeling horrible.

I couldn't stop thinking about Michelle. I wanted to know where she had gone last night and again this morning.

I knew she didn't work until later in the day. I wanted to know if she had really spent the night with Steve. It felt very naïve to believe she hadn't, but I was ready to believe anything. I was kind of hoping Carrie would wake up and tell me not to worry, that nothing happened, we had just gone to sleep ourselves. But I knew no one would tell me anything like what I wanted to hear. I figured Michelle and Steve spent the night together, and now they were going to meet up for lunch. In some months, when the divorce was final, they would be engaged.

It was my day off, only my second since I had started work, but I had two in a row – Saturday and Sunday – which had sounded great until I lay in my room that morning, knowing I would have to spend much of that time with myself, unable to shut off my brain. All I wanted was to go into work, and not think until I was tired enough to go to sleep. Then I remembered Michelle and Carrie would be there, Steve too. This thought made me ill, which in turn made me feel very tired. Finally, I fell back asleep.

9.

I spent most of my two days off from work in bed. When I saw Michelle late on Sunday evening, nothing was weird. We made small talk, and she talked about a movie she was going to see later with some friends, but she didn't invite me along, and she didn't mention the other night. I did not think much of it except for that she seemed almost careful not to mention it. Still, nothing was uncomfortable, so I was sure she didn't know about Carrie and me. And somehow, talking to her, I got the impression she hadn't even slept with Steve. Nothing she said, but it was something in the way she carried herself that told me.

Nothing was weird with Carrie either. I had seen her twice. Once on Saturday, when I finally got out of bed to make myself something to eat, she had just come home from work. She grinned at me very big, but did not mention what had happened.

Are you just now getting out of bed? she asked.

Kind of – I felt pretty bad all day.

Sleepyhead!

Yeah.

We drank a lot last night.

I know.

I talked to Steve, though, she said. He wants you to train all day Monday for the floor.

Who's going to expedite Monday night?

He said he'd hired someone else. He wants you serving.

Right on.

I know, aren't you excited?

Hell yeah, I'll make some money finally.

Maybe you can start saving to go back to school.

I don't know, Carrie.

C'mon, you know you're too good to wait tables.

What's so bad about people who wait tables?

You know what I mean.

I also saw her again on Sunday, but avoided talking to her. I went out for a long walk that afternoon and ended up in Briarwood. I had an early dinner at a bar I knew to have pretty decent food, then drank a couple of beers before walking back. I went to bed early, so I would be well rested for Monday. Not that I cared that much, it just seemed like something to do to keep out of trouble.

The next morning, I woke up, made coffee and toast, read the paper, and was still 15 minutes early for work. Steve was sitting at the bar when I came in. He called me over.

So you're going to train all day today, he said. And tomorrow we'll give you some tables. I know you're itching to make some money. Carrie said you were trying to get money together to go back to school.

Yeah?

Yeah, and I think that's admirable man. I want to help you out, so I'm going to get you on the floor as soon as possible. Just give me one more day to show me you understand the computers and all of that.

No problem, man. Thanks.

I couldn't believe I was talking to the same guy.

Oh, he said. And maybe, in a couple of weeks, when you're comfortable serving, we'll train you for the bar – I know Michelle's tired of working all the time, and I've got a lot going on also. Not to mention Carrie's leaving, so her shifts are open too.

Sounds great.

There's money to be made around here, man. Hang with us.

Sure thing.

I worked all that day feeling pretty good. Michelle came in later and worked the bar with Steve backing her up. He let her leave early in the evening because she was supposed to drive out to the country to visit her mom. It was Monday night and slow, so I sat at the bar drinking my shift beer and talking with Steve. We talked about basketball. There was a college game on TV.

I didn't think you followed sports.

I don't really, I told him. College basketball is different. I grew up watching it.

I like college sports better, too.

Yeah, not everybody's trying to be a damn superstar.

Right on.

The game on TV was Duke and another team, and we watched it intently even though it was a blowout. Duke was always a good team to watch because they were always solid, and they worked well together as a team. I sat there thinking about it, they didn't even know what a rebuilding year was. I thought it sounded like a good thing to say, so I said so to Steve.

Yeah, he said. They're the team to beat.

I didn't leave until the game was over. Steve had even given me another beer while I sat there watching. I felt good about Steve for a change and was looking forward to the coming weeks. Who needs women anyway, I told myself.

When I got home, Carrie was sitting on the front porch.

Hey! she said, as I came up the walk.

What's going on?

Just hanging out... I started my new job today.

Oh, that's right. How did it go?

Great. I love it, they're so nice there.

That's great.

And I'm going to be making so much money, now.

That's wonderful, really.

Yeah, she said. I was even thinking that maybe if you wanted to go back to school this summer or something, I could give you a loan.

I looked away from her. The suggestion made me almost blind with rage. I swallowed it with a deep breath.

Only if you want to – I'm not trying to make you feel bad.

No, no thanks, I said. It probably won't be necessary. I've got a section starting tomorrow, and Steve said he was going to train me for bar in a couple of weeks.

It's about time.

What?

Oh, nothing. It's just he said that he would a week ago. Did you –

I didn't say anything. We were just talking, and I told him about your plans to go back to school, and he said you were a good worker, and he wanted to help you out.

I knew she had though. I couldn't prove it, but I knew she was behind it, and it made me angry. I kept it in, though.

Sit with me, she said, changing the subject. Help me drink this bottle of wine.

I have to work in the morning.

Me too, she said. C'mon, it's red wine. It's good, too.

I don't know, it's probably a bad idea.

You'll like it, c'mon... I even brought a glass out in case you came home.

I knew where it was leading, but I sat anyway. I had been feeling so good and now, knowing she had talked to Steve, I felt rotten again. I did not want to think for myself, so I sat down. She filled the other glass, and I sipped it. It was decent wine, I could tell, but it didn't taste right. I drank it quickly, and she refilled my glass. I tried to drink the second one slower, so I could enjoy it, but it didn't help a whole lot.

Can I tell you something? she asked.

Sure, I said.

You promise you won't be mad?

I don't know, I'm not sure I can promise that.

It's nothing too bad.

I guess.

I told Michelle about us.

What?

I knew it. You're mad.

No, I said.   It's just – that's not what I was expecting you to say.

You don't care?

Well, I mean, I wish you hadn't...

I knew it, she said. You like her.

No, not necessarily –

You like her, and I ruined it for you both.

No, it's just – what did she say?

She said I should go for it.

Go for it?

Yeah.

Go for what?

Look, I know we live together and all, she said. But I think we have a good time together, and when you fucked me... G*d, I loved it. Didn't you like it too?

Sure, I said, and it wasn't the right thing to say, but it didn't matter. She wasn't listening, and she knew that no matter what I said, my indifference wouldn't matter if she didn't listen. We would still end up in bed.

I love it, too.

I'm glad, I said. I didn't really know what to say.

Take me inside.

Now?

Take me inside and fuck me, she said.

We got up and went inside. We went to her room. We would always go to her room if I could help it. I thought that by not going to mine, I could somehow keep her from ever getting too close.

Then, we were naked, and I was taking her from behind on the floor. She was screaming for me to fuck her as I went in and out of her. I was simultaneously in ecstasy and repulsed.

I thought about her telling Michelle about us, whatever the fuck that was – and about her telling Steve to give me a chance at the bar. I thought about that, and the anger came back, and I hated her.

I hated her, so I fucked her harder.

Oh, yes! Harder, baby!

I slammed into her, hoping to hurt her, but I couldn't, and the sick thing was I could not stop the pleasure. The hatred heightened the intensity, and it made for a sickening climax.

For her.

As she was about to come, she turned around and made me take her face-to-face.

Don't come inside me, she said. I forgot to take my pill the other day.

Okay, I said and kept at her.

Oh, G*d! she shouted. You can come on my chest though.

Fine, I breathed.

Or hell, I don't care come inside me!

The hell I would. It was sex. There was nothing pretty or romantic about it at all. Wet, sticky, smelly get-your-rocks-off sex and nothing more, and it would be a sad way to conceive a child.

Still, as she screamed in climax, I was set to do it, and I kept pushing up deeper inside of her. I felt her shudder, and I had to slow to catch my breath.

C'mon, baby, c'mon, she said.

I kept trying, but I couldn't do it.

Come on, baby! She breathed.

But it was no use. I was feeling less and less. I stopped and rolled off of her. I didn't look at her.

I'm sorry, she said. I'm sorry I couldn't get you there.

It's fine, I'm just drunk.

Really?

Yes, I said. I'm drunk.

10.

That was Monday night. I worked Tuesday and made almost $200 for the entire day. I had Wednesday off and I was scheduled for another double shift on Thursday. Steve had Carrie working at the bar until her two weeks were up, so I was taking her place in the dining room during the days. I avoided Carrie after Monday and barely saw her until Thursday night.

I had just come back from my break after the lunch shift, and Steve was sitting at the bar talking to Carrie who was behind it. Carrie left to go wait on a customer. I went up and sat with Steve.

What's up man? I asked him. He was looking at the books.

He looked up and smiled.

Not much, he said. I'm trying to get this shit done, so I can get out early.

Big plans?

Not really – just going to have a drink with Michelle when she gets back in town.

Oh, yeah?

Yeah, she's been helping me through some shit. How about you? You make money today?

All right, I said. Tuesday was bank, though.

Cool, man. Don't worry, Thursday lunches aren't the best, but tonight will be good, and you'll be glad for the supplement when it's all said and done.

Yeah, I'm not worried, I said, feeling grateful to him despite my feelings towards Michelle. It's just good to be working again.

That's good to hear, man. You're getting the hang of things too.

Yeah?

Yeah, he said. I was kind of worried about you at first. Hell, honestly, I was going to let you go, but Carrie said you were a good guy.

She did?

Yeah, she fought tooth and nail for you, man. She's the one who said I needed to put you on the floor.

Oh.

Yeah, but it's cool. Everything's working out for the best. Keep up the good work. He slapped my back and winked at me. Now go clock in.

I went around back to the time clock and stood in front of it. *Everything was working out for the best, my ass.* To hell with Steve if he couldn't see my value on his own, and to hell with Carrie for thinking I wanted or needed her help. And to hell with the other one if she couldn't see that the thing with Steve would turn out to be just like the thing with his wife. People just end up repeating the same patterns over and over and they never see it, especially if they have no reason to change.

I walked back around by Steve, who was still at the bar.

Where you going, man?

To my car, I said, walking out the front door. I'll be right back.

11.

A month later, I went up to admissions to see what it would take to get back in school by summer semester. Carrie was going to loan me the money, and she said I could pay her back when I found a job. Michelle had moved out, so Carrie was also paying the rent each month too.

I had a check at Park Bench, but I could not bring myself to get it. I felt stupid about quitting so easily and thought now that it was a good job in spite of the people. But it was too late to do anything about it, so I told myself it was a good opportunity to get back in school—especially with Carrie letting me borrow the money.

As far as getting a job went, she didn't seem too worried about that. She never told me how much she made as a paralegal, but I know that it was good money, more than she had ever made before. She had tried to keep working at Park Bench on nights and weekends for extra money, but got tired of it quickly. From what I could tell, she hadn't even been missing the extra money.

Hey, baby, she said as I walked in the door to the house.

She was sitting on the couch, drinking a glass of white wine. It was the afternoon, and she had just gotten home, so she was still in her work clothes.

She looked nice.

I sat down next to her. She leaned over and kissed me on the cheek. I forced a smile.

How did it go? she asked.

They're doing registration for the mini-semester, so all the lines in all the offices I needed to go to were a mile long.

I'm sorry.

I can't imagine what it's like in the regular semester. I was talking to this girl standing in one of the lines with me, and she said enrollment was up by some crazy percentage.

You were making friends? She sounded hopeful. I think she was looking for any sign at all that I might be excited about going back to school.

No.

Grumpy! She leaned over, turned my face to hers, and kissed me on the lips. I started to pull back, but she held me to her and put her tongue in my mouth. I kissed her back.

Mmm, she said. So what did they say?

At school? Well, there's good news and bad news.

Oh no! What's the bad news?

I've been out so long, I might have to reapply.

What's the good news?

I might not have to go back to school any time soon?

She gave me this fake, mad look that was supposed to be cute. It made me kind of sick. I was being an asshole and a bum and she needed to get angry with me. She needed to threaten to kick me out on my ass. So what if I was sleeping in her room even when we didn't have sex? She must have seen what was happening. On some level, even I knew.

I don't know, I said finally. I'm going in tomorrow to another office where I can supposedly talk to someone who can help.

That's good.

Yeah, I'm going to go early so there's no line, and then I'm going to go out and look for a job.

That's great, sweetie, but don't burn yourself out.

I need a job. I owe you a lot of money, and it's only accruing while I have no income.

We're doing okay. We've got plenty of money.

No, you've got plenty of money.

It's not like that. Just then, Stanley poked his head around the corner and started crying.

Hey, baby, Carrie called to him. You hungry?

The fat cat cried again.

Is mama's boy hungry? Come over here.

The fat cat came over and tried to jump up on the couch. He couldn't make it the first time, and Carrie nudged me in the arm to help.

He walked over and stood in my lap and pushed his head into me. If Carrie had not been there, I would have pushed him away, but I tried to make a show of liking him when she was around. It was hard. He had gotten worse and worse over the last month.

Maybe it was because he no longer had Ming to pick on, but he woke me up every morning crying until I would give him some wet food. I knew Carrie fed him when she left for work, but I suppose it's hard work staying that fat, and it made him hungry.

He camped out by the door constantly. I would have thought it would have been better once the other cat was gone, but it wasn't. Every time I went outside, he would try to slip out the door.

At first, I would jump after him and grab him as hard as I could and fling him back inside. I thought the suddenness of it all would scare him into not doing it anymore, but it didn't. One time it made me so angry I grabbed him and kept a hold of him as I carried him back inside by the skin around the back of his neck. He screeched and cried and pawed at me with his clawless feet as I stared at him in a fit of anger. I held him and thought of horrible things I could do to him without leaving any marks. Finally, I realized that he was a worthless cat, and that there was little point to it.

Another time, I put the masking tape on his paws and watched him try to walk around. A couple of times, I would put a sock over his head and watch him bumble around like an idiot. Once, I even trapped him under a big waste basket in the bathtub and started running the water. I took him out long before it was dangerous, but it was funny to think about what was going through his head.

I wanted to teach him not to try to get out when I was late for an interview, or not to get under my feet when I was cooking dinner, or not to wake me up in the mornings for a second breakfast. But that is absurd, I know, you can't teach under the threat of punishment, not mention he was just a fucking cat. I was just being cruel because he disgusted me, and I knew it. But I couldn't stop.

Awww, Carrie said, watching me scratch behind his ears. My two boys.

All right, enough, I said to the cat. I took my hand away.

Will you do me a favor? She finished her glass of wine and stood up.

Sure.

Feed Stanley for me? I've got to go meet Michelle. I won't be back too late. Give him wet food. He's been a good boy.

Yeah, I said. I'll do it in a second, when I get up to make a drink.

She frowned at me.

What?

Nothing, she said. Just don't get drunk.

I'm just going to have one, maybe two.

I know. I just worry about you when you drink alone.

I'm fine, though. I've always done it – whiskey's good for thinking.

I know, it makes you happy.

And if I do get drunk, I'm not a mean drunk.

That's true, she said. She leaned down, kissed Stanley, then me. She smiled. Just don't get too drunk. You know what I mean?

Yeah.

I love you, she said.

I looked at her. It was the third time she had told me that. Both times, I had not answered her.

I love you, too, I said finally.

She kissed me and left to go meet Michelle, presumably up at Park Bench. I thought about it and thought it would be nice to be able to go back up there. I thought it would be nice to see Michelle, that it would be nice to see anyone. I was depressed and had not been out in weeks.

I thought maybe I needed to give some friends a call and get out of the house. But then I thought you can't really call people up and ask them to buy you drinks, and that made me sick of thinking, so I got up to make myself one.

I went into the kitchen and got a glass from over the sink. I poured a finger's worth of whiskey into the glass and drank it down. I poured another one, a little bigger. Then I fed Stanley. I took a can from the pantry, opened it, and put it in his bowl by the refrigerator.

He started eating like he had not eaten in weeks.

I sipped my drink, leaning against the counter, watching him. He hardly stopped to breathe. When he was done, he looked up and made a noise at me. The whole scene made me sick inside. In all my life, I had never seen anything so pathetic.

Back when I lived near Piedmont Park, I was walking one morning, and I met this woman who was drinking a twelve-pack of Steel Reserve at nine o'clock in the morning down by the lake. She had told me I was cute as I walked by and offered me one. I thought it would be funny to sit and have a beer with her.   From the way she talked she was probably in her forties, maybe fifties, but she looked much older. She had long gray hair, slick and tangled and she was missing teeth. Her clothes were too big for her frame, she was mostly skeletal with a thin layer of liver-spotted skin stretched across it. She smoked menthols incessantly.

She was a panhandler. She told me she had once made 600 dollars begging. She spent most of the money she made on crack cocaine and beer, but with social security she managed to have enough for a place to live.

She said she had just kicked her boyfriend out, who had been a male prostitute. They had gotten into a fight because she asked him for part of the rent, and he called her a whore. She told me how her ex-husband had once beaten her over the head with a brick. She had two sons in the military, one in the army, the other in the air force, neither of whom she ever saw. They sent her money occasionally.

When I had finished my beer, I stood up to go. Out of nowhere, she asked me if I knew what it was I needed. She had a thick Tennessee drawl.

What's that? I crushed my beer can and tossed it in the trash can nearby.

Peace of mind, she said. I used to feel guilty about it, telling people I was homeless when I got a place to stay, when I get a check. But then I found peace of mind. It's the most important thing in the world.

Yeah, I guess so.

I look at you, and I think, he needs some peace of mind. She stood up and walked over to me.

I looked at her, trying to figure out what she meant.

I could help you find it. She reached up and started to pull me towards her.

I turned my head, pulled away from her.

Let's meet up on Tuesday when my check comes. We'll get a beer and a couple rocks, spend the day.

That's all right, I said. Maybe some other time.

For a long time after, I wondered what kind of man would have stayed. Then, I wondered if maybe I had her wrong. Maybe she knew something I didn't know. Maybe she knew some kind of spiritual truth that would have set me free, like her, had I simply let her whisper it in my ear. That thought, as unlikely as it is, has stayed with me through the years, even when nothing else has.

There was something beautiful about her life to me. It kind of reminded me of weeds growing out from cracks in the sidewalk, life finding a way at any cost. I wished I could learn to be happy with so little. But watching Stanley took something away from all of that. It made me wonder if a life like his could ever be worth the cost. At least the woman on the street was free. At least she could fend for herself, even if it was by begging. After all she had been through, she was still scraping by without answering to anyone. There was a certain respect I could have for someone who could suspend their pride in order to scrape by.

To some degree, that was Stanley, but he did more than scrape by, he prospered, and prosperity is only respectable when it is on the work of the person who is prospering. Stanley traded everything for his. Stanley was just another fat ass living off the fat of the land.

I took the rest of my drink, poured another.

I needed a change of scenery. It had been a nice day out. It was a little hot in the afternoon, but by now, it would have cooled off. I decided to take my drink outside, away from Stanley.

I sat my drink on the dining room table and went to the bathroom to take a leak. I caught a glimpse of myself in the mirror. I had gained a few pounds. I would have to get back into the routine of jogging once I was finally settled in wherever it was I landed.

I pissed, then headed to the front door. Stanley was waiting.

He cried once, and I felt a flood of rage rush over me. I wanted to pick him up and take his head in my hand and twist his neck. Put him out of his misery. I threw my glass against the far wall, and it smashed into pieces, leaving a dent in the plaster. Stanley shrank back against the door.

Then the rage subsided, and all I had was pity.

You want out?

He looked up, his eyes huge with terror.

You want out? Fine, go out.

I went over and opened the door. At first, he started to run off.

Wait, boy, c'mon Stanley.

I coaxed him to the door, and then seeing it open, he ran out. I leaned my head against the open door and took a deep breath.

I felt a release. I knew he wouldn't come back. No cat would ever come back to a place where it was so trapped. I would just tell Carrie he got out, and there was nothing I could do.

I looked up and saw him still on the porch. He just stood there, looking out. The sun was going down behind the houses and the trees across the street, and with the multitude of colors created by the sunset mixing with the air pollution, it was a beautiful night.

Go on, I shouted.

He looked back at me, then he looked back out. He lied down on the porch.

The anger returned.

I breathed slowly, deeply—then walked back into the house, leaving the door open. I went to the bathroom and looked at myself in the mirror. I screamed, tugging at the hair above my temples. I wanted to smash my own face in the mirror. I went back to where Stanley was sitting on the porch. I picked him up, and he screeched. I pulled him to my chest.

It's okay, buddy, I said. It's all going to be okay.

I took him out to my car and opened the passenger door. He purred in bewilderment as I put him in. I walked around and got in the driver's side, started the car.

I took him across town, past Briarwood Drive and into a nice neighborhood. I took the tag off of his collar and got out and went around and opened the passenger side door with the car running. I picked him up and sat him on the street. He tried to get back in the car, but I blocked his way, and closed the door. I went around and got back in the driver's seat.

It's okay, buddy. It's for the best, I said.

I watched him in the passenger side mirror as I drove off. When I pulled back onto Briarwood, I realized I was crying. I drove around for an hour or more, trying to clear my head, get my story straight. It was around 10 pm when I got home. Carrie was there. I walked inside, and she was standing between the living room and dining room.

Where have you been? Where's Stanley? she asked. And why was there a broken glass and whiskey all over the floor?

I lost it, I told her. I threw it at the wall when he got out. I chased him for a block or two, through the yards, but I couldn't catch him.

Oh, G*d.

I've been driving around looking for him for two hours, but I couldn't find him. He's gone.

Have you been crying? she asked.

Look, I'm so sorry, I told her. I know how much he means to you.

It's okay, it's okay, she said taking me in her arms. We'll find him. You probably just went too far. He probably doubled back and is in the backyard.

But I could tell by her voice that she was worried.

We went out and looked until after midnight. Finally, we gave up, went inside, and went to bed. When the lights were out, I felt the bed start to shake, and I realized she was crying. I rolled over, tried to hold her, but she pushed me away.

12.

The fat cat came back the next day, but Carrie was at work. I told her I would spend the day looking for him, which seemed to make her feel a little better. Instead, I went out and had breakfast with the last of my money. I ate a big breakfast at a diner down the street and tried not to think about the cat. I read the paper while I ate, and when I was done, I felt nice and full, so I asked the waitress for more coffee and finished reading the paper in the diner.

When I got back home, he was standing on the porch by the door. We watched each other for a little bit. I tried to figure out how he could have found his way back.

But he was not going to get off that easy. I knew there was a better life out there, and I was sure he could find it. I picked him up off the porch and put him back in the car, and this time I took him twice as far in a different direction. I drove him up to a nice neighborhood in the suburbs, the one where my ex-girlfriend had grown up and lived for a while with her mother while we were together. I let him out around the corner from her childhood house, wondering at the significance.

C'mon, now, I told him. You're free. Live it up.

I got back to the house and read for a while on the couch. Then, sick of being lazy, I got up and took a walk. It worked out well because I got home right as Carrie was driving up.

Have you been looking all this time? she said.

Yeah, I told her. No luck.

We went inside and made dinner. We ate in silence, and after eating, she said she wanted to take a walk to clear her head.

Maybe if he sees me, he'll come out, she said.

I sat on the sofa feeling awful. I wanted some way to make her feel better, so I went into my bedroom and sat down at the computer. We had hooked it up back in that room after Michelle had left. Carrie never seemed to use it, so I didn't feel like she was infringing on my space.

At the computer, I typed up fliers saying LOST CAT with our information on it and with Stanley's name and description. When she got home, I told her I would print up a bunch of copies tomorrow and post them all over town. She hugged me, and I held her for a while. We went to bed early.

The next day, I left at the same time as Carrie and went over to the copy place and made copies of the fliers. I hung them up around our neighborhood and even over around Briarwood so Carrie would see them while she was out. I figured it would give her hope while she got used to the idea of living without him.

As ridiculous as it sounds, when I got home, I half-expected to see Stanley there, waiting on the porch. But he wasn't, so I breathed easier. I told myself that he had found a new home, a better home, where they would let him outside and he could hunt rats and chipmunks and squirrels. I saw him in my head, already a couple of pounds lighter.

Looking good, Stan, I said out loud. Looking good.

The next day, I went back over to school and stood in line. I told Carrie that I could not spend anymore days looking for Stanley, and that if he were around someone would call. I was lucky and caught one of the assistant deans of admissions coming back from lunch. I apparently made some impression on her, because she said she would make a couple of calls, so maybe I wouldn't have to reapply. She gave me a card and told me to email her next week.

Carrie and I got in around the same time. I told her the news, hoping it would cheer her up.

That's great, babe, Carrie said. Anybody call about Stanley?

No, I said.

Then it occurred to me. I thought that it was very likely that someone would call, and it would turn out to be a false alarm. I thought it would be horrible for Carrie if she got her hopes up so high only to have them dashed.

What is it? she asked.

Well, I wasn't going to mention it...

What?

I got one call, but it was a false alarm. I went over, and it wasn't him.

Oh.

I'm sorry. I'm afraid we might get a bunch of those before we find him.

Do you think we'll find him?

I don't know.

I went out job hunting the next day, but didn't come across anything that seemed worthwhile. I had a beer at a bar around three o'clock. When I came home, Stanley was sitting on the front porch. At first, I didn't recognize him. He had lost weight and was looking leaner. He did not look sickly or like he had lost too much too fast, so I figured he must have gotten food somewhere. I shook my head and smiled. I couldn't believe he found his way back.

I looked at my watch, realized I only had an hour or so before Carrie would be home. I picked him up and brought him out to the car a third time. I tried to figure out how he kept finding his way home. I could not take him quite as far into the suburbs, there wasn't enough time, not with rush hour traffic. But as he bounced around the floor of the passenger seat, I found a neighborhood and drove around in circles, hoping to disorient him. I let him out and drove quickly home. I just barely beat Carrie there. She didn't like it if I was not there when she got home, especially if I didn't leave a note.

The next week was very uneasy for me, because despite the precautions I had taken, I was afraid Stanley would show up again. Not to mention I had not been able to find a job. I came home everyday feeling defeated, expecting him to be sitting on the porch waiting for me. I still felt trapped.

One day, I don't remember how long after, I woke up and didn't go out looking for a job at all. I woke up and started drinking. Not a habit I practiced often, but I just felt like being numb on that particular day.

So I woke up and drank the rest of a six pack I had in the refrigerator. When that was gone, I felt pretty good, so I sat around watching TV. Around lunch time, I started to make something to eat, but I wasn't hungry. So I opened a bottle of Carrie's wine instead. It was a blush wine, kind of sweet, but it was the only thing there was to drink in the entire house besides whiskey, and there was something about drinking whiskey in the daytime that seemed too depraved.

I spent the day drunk.

At around half past four, I must have drifted off for a minute, because I was startled awake when the phone rang. I jumped up, answered it.

Hello?

Hi, I'm calling because I think I might have found Stanley. It was a woman's voice.

I don't think that's possible, I said.

You found him already?

Yeah, I said quickly. Yeah, we did. Thank you, though.

I hung up the phone. It rang again a minute later.

Hello?

Hey, it's me.

Oh, hey.

I was calling to let you know, I'll be home in about 15 minutes. I'm stopping to get some groceries.

Just then, I heard a scratching at the door. Or not so much a scratching, but something like it. My heart sank.

That clawless fat fuck, I said, covering the receiver with my palm.

Huh?

Oh, nothing, babe. Yeah, c'mon home. I'll be here.

I hung up the phone and ran to the door. I opened it, and there he was.

I wondered for a minute if I was crazy. It didn't seem possible. I didn't know what to do, Carrie would be home soon. I thought about just letting him in, of the merry homecoming it would make. She wouldn't even be mad that I had been drinking all day. We would eat dinner, then go to bed, probably have sex. It sounded almost nice. We hadn't had sex since I had first freed Stanley. The problem was that I would wake up the next day feeling like shit.

I put my leg out to keep him from getting inside. I picked him up and took him out to the car. There was a note in Carrie's handwriting sitting on the dash: I'm proud of you, it said. And she had drawn a flower.

I ran back inside, grabbed the cell phone Carrie had gotten for me. I knew she would be calling me when she got home, and I wasn't there.

I got in the car, turned the engine on, started driving. The only problem was that I didn't know where to take him. I knew he would only come back if I left him out in the world on his own. He was like everyone else. He wanted to pay lip service to being free when he saw others that were free, like Ming. But at the end of the day, he knew where his wet food was waiting. And being a fat ass do-nothing wasn't so bad if you got wet food every day, sometimes twice a day.

Carrie had loaned me fifty bucks, so I could eat lunch while out searching for jobs. I stopped off at a liquor store and bought a pint of whiskey. Then I went to a gas station and filled up. I took sips of whiskey while the tank was filling. The cell phone had been ringing off the hook.

The gas station I stopped at was just off an exit on I-20, which runs east to west through the city. I saw a billboard that advertised fireworks for sale the next state over. *Only 75 miles west to the state line!* Fireworks were illegal in Georgia, and the sign said it was the closest place that sold them.

I thought about taking Stanley across state lines.

Still, I knew he'd be back. I could ship him to fucking Zimbabwe, and this fucker would never let me have any peace.

The phone rang again, I picked it up.

Where are you? Carrie shouted frantically.

Nowhere, I said, feeling drunk.

Nowhere?

I didn't answer.

She said my name.

No answer.

Are you there?

Yeah.

Why did you tell my friend Shelly that you had found Stanley when she called?

That was the best. It had been a set up. Or maybe Shelly had just found a cat that looked like Stanley and called. I had a hard time imagining Carrie as being that suspicious, even as much as I hated her.

His tag, she said. I found his tag in the floorboard of your car when I left the note.

I drank some more whiskey, realized just how easy it was to get out of this. All I had to do was tell her I had him in the car – that I had found the tag out yesterday, spent the day leaving flyers on the doorstep in the neighborhood where I found it. Someone had called when I got home, not five minutes before Shelly did. I knew it had to be him by the description of his suit jacket and his mustache. *His what?* she would say, and I would explain, and we'd laugh – I'd go home, we'd eat and fuck and I'd still wake up feeling like shit the next day. Hell, maybe it could work out. Maybe I wouldn't even feel like shit if I quit drinking, found a job, went to school – changed something. But I knew, one day, somewhere down the line, I would wake up, and it would be there, staring me in the face. Stanley would be standing in the doorway of the bedroom, crying for his second breakfast, only to eat it before going to sit by the door.

Oh, G*d, I said, finally. I didn't want to tell you, I didn't know how. I found him the other day by the side of the road.

What do you mean?

I didn't want to hurt you, I said. Or maybe I was just afraid you would hate me because I was the one who let him out.

What do you mean you found him?

He's dead, Carrie.

But that's impossible.

No, I said. It's true, I'm sorry.

But...

I could tell she was starting to cry.

Look, I feel like shit, I – I need some time away.

What? What are you talking about?

Look, I can't deal with the way I'm feeling right now.

But, Stanley, what about...

I'm going to stay with a friend for a few days. I'll call you when I'm in a better state of mind.

Wait.

I'm so sorry...

I hung up the phone.

I pulled out of the gas station, got on the highway, headed west. The cell phone started ringing again. I rolled down the window and threw it out. I reached over, scratched Stanley behind his ears. I had no idea where I was going. It was getting dark now, the sun setting quickly, and on the horizon, I swear I saw fireworks – just like it was the Fourth of July.

-ACKNOWLEDGEMENTS-

Thanks for the cover goes to the amazing Leah Hale. Her website is LeahHale.com. Images used are credited to: Photos by Ingridi Alves Photograph and Zhang Kaiyy on Unsplash. Thanks to Mike Ruther, my long time editor, attorney (though he's never passed a bar), and angel/devil on my shoulder.

The title story here has some clear nods to Lenny Bruce and some allusions to his great autobiography *How To Talk Dirty and Influence People*. Thanks to S.G. for the anecdote which inspired *Any Constellation*, though most of the felonies were added by me. I hope I didn't abuse the premise too much by aligning it to the story I ultimately decided to tell. Further, thank you to the various literary journals which have published my stories to date: The Alabama Literary Review, The Bayou Review, The Crab Orchard Review, Harpur Palate, Phoebe, and The Rubbertop Review.

Finally, thanks to Della Taylor, my wife and partner, for the time and humor she has donated to my writing, and most of all, for her example of the faith that it takes to let a grown man invite his perversity and cynicism in order to make-believe that at the center of such baseness (such as is related here) there is also something of the purity of the human spirit resembled. For a while it seemed acceptable inspiration to simply assign the worst possible intentions to myself and those I knew and call it art. Untrue, I realize, in retrospect, but art or no, I have never doubted these stories to be fictional and bearing no resemblance to persons living or dead beyond the coincidental. In the apophatic tradition, G*d (if you believe in that sort of thing) is considered ineffable and unimaginable and so must be defined by what characteristics He is not. Love of friends, partners, and family is at the heart of this text as much as anything else, even if the best of that love is emphasized more by its absence than presence. Thus, I believe, this book is in fact a form of praise.

You can follow me on twitter @brent_fiction and on facebook @brenttaylorfiction or visit my website: brenttaylorfiction.com.